FOUR IDIOTS AND A HAUNTED MANSION

FLIRTING IN THE FACE OF DEATH

SAM SCARE

To everyone who's ever said,
"What's the worst that could happen?"
and then immediately found out.

To the friends who make you laugh in the dark,
fight ghosts with sarcasm,
and stick around even when reality glitches.

And most of all...
to Jake —
the idiot who proved that even in death,
you can still be the funniest one in the group.

Contents

Foreword

Welcome to the wonderfully wicked world of Four Idiots and a Haunted Mansion. This book isn't your average haunted house story—unless your idea of "average" includes a sarcastic ghost, cursed toilets, flirty disasters, and a group of teens with the survival instincts of a soggy sock.

Written with equal parts spooky suspense and ridiculous humor, this horror-comedy dives headfirst into chaos when four not-so-brilliant friends stumble into a mansion no one dares to enter. What follows is a cocktail of jump scares, laugh-out-loud moments, awkward crushes, and ghostly tantrums that will leave you grinning while gripping the edge of your seat.

If you're the kind of reader who likes your chills served with giggles, and your romance awkward and hilarious, then turn the page. You're about to meet Jake, Sophie, Max, and Sarah—the brave, the dumb, and the occasionally possessed.

Enjoy the madness. But remember... never trust a haunted toilet.
—The Author

PROLOGUE

Meet the Idiots: A Survival Guide (You're Gonna Need It)

~ Jake – The "Leader" (because someone had to be)
Confident? Yes. Competent? Debatable. Jake's the guy who says "trust me" right before everything explodes. Armed with a backpack full of snacks and zero survival instincts, he's convinced every haunted creak is just "bad plumbing." Surprisingly good at dodging ghosts—mostly by running faster than the others.

~Sophie – The Sass Queen with a Sixth Sense (for drama)
Witty, stylish, and always ready with a snarky comeback, Sophie treats haunted mansions like runway catwalks. She'll roast a demon and flirt with danger—literally. If sarcasm was a weapon, she'd be untouchable. Warning: do not mess with her hair... or her crush.

~ Max – The Muscles and the Mayhem
Max is strong, brave, and completely unaware that ghosts don't respond to flexing. If "punch first, ask questions never" was a strategy, he invented it. He's got the heart of a hero, the brain of a potato chip, and the attention span of a goldfish on espresso.

~ Sarah – The Brainiac Who's So Over This
Smart, skeptical, and always five seconds away from quitting the group, Sarah is the only one who read the haunted warning sign. Twice. She's fluent in ghost lore, Latin curses, and rolling her eyes. Somehow, she keeps the team alive—with science, logic, and deep sighs of disappointment.

Together, they're the perfect disaster. One haunted mansion. Four chaotic teens. Zero clue what they're doing. Let the haunting (and the stupidity) begin! ???

I

The Jungle Detour That Ruined Everything

"Can everyone please shut up for five minutes?" Mr. Allen barked from the front of the school bus, clutching his clipboard like it was a grenade.

That had absolutely no effect.

The bus was chaos—screaming, laughing, loud music from wireless speakers, someone throwing chips across the aisle, and at least one kid pretending to die dramatically for no apparent reason. The seniors of Redwood High were heading on their final school trip, and the entire ride felt like a jungle gym on wheels.

Jake leaned back in his seat near the back, legs stretched out, hoodie halfway zipped, earbuds in but not playing anything. He wasn't listening to music—he was eavesdropping. Much more fun.

"You know what would make this trip bearable?" he said aloud without looking.

"Losing your voice?" came Sophie's dry reply. She sat in the seat across from him, book in hand, hair in a messy bun, and about 60% done pretending she didn't like talking to Jake.

Jake grinned. "A haunted castle. Full of traps. Ghosts. Maybe some secret treasure."

Max, lounging behind them with his hoodie pulled over his face like a burrito, peeked out. "Bro, it's a forest preserve. You're not Indiana Jones. The only thing we'll find out there is bugs. And disappointment."

Sarah, who sat next to Max and was sketching something in her notebook, added with a smirk, "And poison ivy. Don't forget that romantic part."

"Oh please," Jake said, sitting up and dramatically motioning at the window. "Look at that jungle! There could be anything in there. Lost civilizations. Cursed ruins. Bigfoot."

Sophie snorted. "This is not a movie, Jake. It's a school-sponsored picnic."

Jake smirked. "Oh, I'm sorry. I forgot we're all here to bond with nature and write poems about leaves."

"I like poems," Sarah said, not looking up from her sketch. "And leaves."

Max patted her shoulder. "You also thought the scarecrow in that Halloween maze was 'cute.' I rest my case."

The bus hit a bump and half the students screamed like they were being launched into space. Mr. Allen rubbed his temples.

Jake twisted in his seat to face his trio of partners in crime—friends by fate, not necessarily choice. They were all weird in their own way, but together they made sense. Like puzzle pieces from four different boxes that somehow managed to click.

"So," he said, lowering his voice into that familiar Jake-tone: half trouble, half charm, all dumb ideas. "How do we make this trip... unforgettable?"

Sophie sighed. "You're planning something, aren't you?"

"Noooo," Jake said, clearly lying. "But if I was, it would involve something way cooler than hiking around with a bunch of future accountants."

Max perked up. "Go on."

Jake pointed out the bus window. Through the blur of green trees and winding dirt paths, there was a glimpse of something odd—an overgrown trail that veered sharply away from the main road. There was a half-broken wooden sign, so faded you couldn't read it, swallowed by vines and time.

"There," Jake said. "That's our detour."

Sophie followed his finger and squinted. "That's not a trail. That's a death wish. Also, it literally says DANGER."

Sarah leaned across Max to see. "What if it's... y'know... just old? Like abandoned? Could be cool."

"You see?" Jake said triumphantly. "She gets it. Adventure! Mystery! Probably rabid squirrels!"

Max sipped his soda and shrugged. "Alright. As long as it's not another fake ghost tour like last time. I still want those three hours of my life back."

Jake gave a wolfish grin. "You're all in."

Sophie groaned. "Why do I always let you drag me into this stuff?"

"Because," Jake said with a wink, "deep down, you love chaos."

She didn't answer, but she definitely didn't say no.

The bus finally pulled to a stop near a forest clearing. Mr. Allen stood, barely restraining his exhaustion. "Everyone out! Group leaders, keep your teams close! Don't wander off, don't touch any wildlife, and for heaven's sake, no couples sneaking away for make-out spots."

Half the bus groaned. Jake leaned toward Sophie and whispered, "Guess we'll have to accidentally get lost instead."

Sophie raised an eyebrow. "You wish."

They grabbed their bags, filed off the bus, and within minutes, students were spreading out over the picnic site. Some were taking selfies with trees, others flopping dramatically onto the grass like they'd hiked Everest.

That's when Jake made his move.

He motioned subtly to the others, and the four of them broke off from the group, ducking behind a hedge, then through a clump of trees, and then—like they were on a secret mission—they slipped into the overgrown trail they'd seen earlier.

The forest swallowed them.

The difference was instant. One step off the main path, and the light dimmed like someone had turned down the sun's volume. The trees grew taller, older, gnarled like knotted hands. The air smelled of wet earth and secrets, and every sound—the rustle of leaves, the snap of a twig—felt louder somehow. Like the forest was paying attention.

"Okay," Sophie muttered, tugging her hoodie closer. "I'll admit. This is... creepier than expected."

Jake turned around, walking backward with a cocky grin. "Told you. Worth it already."

Max swatted a mosquito. "I swear, if this leads to a dead end or a bear den, I'm suing someone."

"It's not like we're that far from the main camp," Sarah said, stepping over a root. "We can find our way back in ten minutes, right?"

Nobody answered immediately.

Then Jake said, "...Sure. Probably."

Sophie narrowed her eyes. "Probably?"

"Relax," Jake said. "I got snacks. I got water. I got—"

"A broken sense of direction," Max finished for him.

They walked deeper, the trail getting thinner and the trees thicker. Vines hung like curtains. The temperature dropped. At some point, the birds stopped singing.

"Okay, has anyone noticed how quiet it's gotten?" Sarah asked softly.

They all paused.

The silence was thick. No birds. No bugs. Not even wind. Just their footsteps, breath, and the pounding suspicion that something wasn't right.

Jake tried to lighten the mood. "Maybe the wildlife's shy. Or on break."

Sophie gave him a look. "Or maybe they know something we don't."

They pushed forward, nervously laughing, trading theories—jungle ghosts, forest witches, government experiments. Max insisted it was just an abandoned hunting trail. Sophie pointed out the clearly human-cut stones partially buried in the ground. Sarah kept glancing at the trees like they were watching.

And then they saw it.

Through the misty veil of branches, something massive loomed ahead. A dark, jagged shape partially hidden by vines and fog.

Jake froze. "No freaking way."

They moved closer, their steps slowing like gravity had thickened around them.

It was a mansion.

Or what was left of one.

The structure stood crooked and half-devoured by nature. Ivy crawled across its stone walls. Shattered windows stared like black, hollow eyes. The gate was twisted iron, rusted and creaking in the faint breeze that had returned only to make things creepier. Moss clung to everything. There were gargoyles—actual stone gargoyles—on the roof, staring down like angry librarians.

Sophie whispered, "That's not a cabin. That's not even a normal old house."

Jake stepped closer, eyes wide with adrenaline. "This is what I'm talking about! Look at it. It's perfect!"

Sarah blinked. "Perfect for what? Contracting tetanus?"

Max stared. "It looks... haunted."

Jake grinned. "Exactly."

Sophie grabbed his arm. "Wait. We're not seriously going in there. Right?"

Jake glanced at the mansion, then at her, then back. "...What if we just look around? You know. For fun. One lap. No big deal."

Sophie stared at him. "You're like a magnet for bad decisions."

"Don't deny it's exciting."

"I'm denying everything."

But as usual, Jake's energy was infectious. Sarah looked fascinated, Max was half-curious-half-terrified, and Sophie... well, she was already following them toward the iron gate, even while muttering, "This is how every horror movie starts."

Jake pushed open the gate.

It groaned like it hadn't moved in a hundred years.

The mansion waited, silent and still, like it had been expecting them.

Inside was worse.

The front door creaked open with a shove. Dust exploded in the air like a sneeze from the past. The foyer was grand once—black marble floors, a spiraling staircase, a chandelier that looked like it would kill anyone standing beneath it.

Cobwebs drooped from every corner. Broken furniture lay in piles. Portraits hung crooked on the walls, their faces faded or scratched out completely. Something skittered across the floor in the shadows. No one wanted to check what.

"I take back everything I said," Sophie whispered. "We should leave. Like, now."

Jake spun in a circle, arms wide. "Are you kidding? This is amazing! This is exactly the adventure we needed!"

Sarah was already taking pictures with her phone. "These are gonna look insane on Insta."

Max shivered. "My spine just signed a resignation letter."

They stepped inside fully, the door creaking shut behind them. The sound echoed down long, dark hallways.

"Okay," Jake said, clapping his hands. "Split up or stick together?"

Sophie: "Stick together."

Max: "Super stick together."

Sarah: "Please stick together. This place gives me the creeps."

Jake: "Group vote wins. Let's explore."

The air inside the mansion felt different. Heavy. Thick, like breathing through a blanket. Every step they took echoed too loudly, like the house didn't like being disturbed. The more they moved, the more they noticed things they wished they hadn't.

A piano missing half its keys but somehow still playing a note now and then. A fireplace full of ashes—but the ashes weren't gray. They were... pinkish. Like melted wax. Or bone.

"Okay, okay," Jake said with a nervous laugh. "Maybe it's a little creepy."

Sophie elbowed him. "You think?"

"I mean, not murder-creepy. Just... ghost-story creepy."

"That's exactly what murderers say before people die."

They passed a massive painting of a family. Mother, father, two kids—all wearing clothes from, like, the 1800s. The weird part? All their eyes had been scratched out.

Sarah stared at it. "That's not disturbing at all."

Max pointed at a trail of muddy footprints going up the stairs. "Guys... those are fresh."

Everyone stopped.

Jake squinted. "Maybe an animal?"

Sophie raised a brow. "What animal wears boots?"

They stood there, frozen. Nobody wanted to say what they were all thinking: someone else had been here. Maybe was still here. Maybe wasn't alive.

A floorboard creaked above them.

They jumped.

Max whispered, "Okay, we're leaving, right? Like right now?"

Jake hesitated. "...Or we go upstairs and find out who it is."

Sophie grabbed his arm. "Do you want to die?"

"I want to know what's up there."

"You've watched too many horror movies."

Jake grinned. "And yet here we are, living one."

Sophie stared at him like she couldn't decide whether to slap him or kiss him.

Sarah looked at Max. "We're going upstairs, aren't we?"

Max sighed. "I blame Jake."

The staircase creaked under their weight. Dust puffed with every step. The chandelier above them swung slightly even though there was no breeze.

Halfway up, they all stopped as something cold brushed against their ankles.

Jake looked down. "Did anyone feel—"

"Yes," all three said at once.

They reached the second floor. The hallway stretched long, with doors on both sides. Some open. Some barely cracked. The wallpaper was peeling, the floor sagging.

At the far end was a tall mirror.

A really, really old one.

Jake walked toward it, drawn to it. "This thing's huge…"

They all approached it slowly.

It was dusty and clouded, the glass warped slightly with age. But their reflections showed up clear enough—though something was… off.

Jake leaned in.

In the reflection, his group stood behind him, but—

Sophie's reflection blinked… a second late.

Max's smiled when he wasn't.

Sarah's had no eyes.

They all gasped and jumped back.

Jake turned around. Everyone looked normal.

They turned back to the mirror.

Normal again.

Sophie's voice shook. "I want that thing smashed."

Jake nodded. "Seconded."

Then the mirror cracked down the middle.

Nobody touched it.

The sound rang like a shriek.

They backed away quickly. Jake tried to joke. "Okay, so the house has… character."

Sarah whispered, "Did you hear that?"

A faint humming. Like a music box. Echoing faintly from one of the nearby rooms.

Max gulped. "Nope. Nope. Nope."

Jake opened the nearest door.

Inside was a nursery.

Tiny rocking chair. Torn wallpaper with teddy bears. A broken crib.

And on the floor, a music box playing on its own.

Sophie stepped back. "I swear if that thing starts flying, I'm gone."

Jake picked it up—and the music stopped.

The box was cold. Too cold. Like touching ice.

He dropped it instantly.

The lid popped open.

Inside was a picture of four kids.

Two boys. Two girls.

They looked... almost exactly like them.

Sarah's face went pale. "That's not funny, Jake."

Jake shook his head. "I didn't put that in there."

Max backed toward the door. "We're leaving. Now."

And then the door slammed shut.

By itself.

The slam echoed through the room, a violent punctuation to their sudden panic.

"Shit," Jake muttered, rattling the door handle. Locked. No budging.

Sarah pressed her back against the door, breathing hard. "This isn't funny anymore."

Max tried the windows—too high and barred by vines. "We're trapped."

Sophie's eyes darted around the nursery like she expected shadows to leap out at any second. "Trapped where? This place feels like a nightmare made of rotten wood."

The music box lay open on the floor between them, its tiny ballerina frozen mid-twirl. The picture inside haunted all four of them, the kids eerily resembling themselves.

Jake's voice cracked. "How is that even possible? That has to be a prank."

Sophie's gaze flickered toward him. "You don't think you did it?"

Jake looked away. "No. Definitely not me."

The room grew colder. The faint hum of the music box started again, slower, deeper, like a lullaby from the bottom of a grave.

Suddenly, the shadows in the corners of the room twisted.

Something moved.

Sophie gasped and backed up, tripping over a rocking horse and hitting the floor hard.

Jake and Max rushed to help her up, but Sarah froze, staring wide-eyed at the far corner.

"Guys..." she whispered, "look."

They turned and saw it—a figure materializing, flickering like a bad TV signal. A little girl, pale and translucent, with long dark hair and hollow eyes.

She smiled.

But it wasn't a happy smile.

It was a warning.

The girl pointed toward the door. Then toward the music box. Then at each of them.

"You don't belong," her voice echoed—soft and broken, like a ghost's sigh.

"Leave," she said.

The room suddenly felt like it was closing in.

Max shouted, "How do we get out?"

The girl vanished. The door unlocked with a loud click.

They bolted out.

Back in the hallway,

breathing hard, hearts pounding like war drums.

"Okay," Jake said, voice trembling. "We need to get out. Now."

Sophie nodded. "Agreed."

But Max shook his head. "Wait. Before we run—we need to understand what that was. Who that girl was. Why the picture looks like us."

Sarah swallowed. "What if... we're not here by accident?"

Jake frowned. "Like, what do you mean?"

"What if this place... knows us?"

Sophie laughed bitterly. "Yeah, right. That's insane."

Max glanced around nervously. "Maybe insane is exactly right."

They made their way through the creaking mansion, deeper and deeper into its cold, forgotten heart.

Rooms whispered secrets. Walls had eyes. The mansion seemed alive and hungry.

At one point, a mirror cracked again as they passed, a shadow flickering behind it.

Sophie shivered, gripping Jake's arm. "This is a nightmare. We should have stayed on the path."

Jake grinned weakly. "At least it's never boring with us."

The mansion's secrets were far from done with them.

The deeper they ventured, the heavier the air became, like the mansion was holding its breath—waiting.

Their footsteps echoed down hallways lined with peeling wallpaper, torn curtains, and eerie portraits whose eyes seemed to follow.

Max stopped abruptly, pointing to a door covered in strange symbols. "What is that?"

Jake shrugged. "Probably something that says Don't Open Me, Ever."

"Yeah, no way," Sophie said firmly.

But Jake, ever the adventurer, was already turning the knob.

The door creaked open to reveal a dusty study filled with books, jars of strange things, and a large wooden desk covered in scattered papers.

Jake flipped on his phone's flashlight and started poking through the papers.

One caught Sophie's eye. It was a faded diary, the cover cracked with age.

"Guys, look at this," she said, opening it carefully.

The diary belonged to someone named Eleanor—dated 1892.

She read aloud, voice low: "The house watches. The house remembers. We tried to leave, but it will not let us go. The children—our children—are trapped forever in its walls."

A chill ran down their spines.

Suddenly, a cold breeze swept the room. The pages of the diary flipped wildly as if caught in a storm.

Jake slammed the book shut.

"Okay, that's enough history lesson," he said. "We need to get out of here."

Suddenly, footsteps echoed above them—slow, deliberate, approaching.

"Who's there?" Sarah called out, voice shaking.

No answer.

The footsteps stopped.

The silence pressed down on them again, suffocating and thick.

Then, a whisper floated down from the ceiling.

"Stay." The word was a ghostly hiss, curling like smoke.

Jake swallowed hard.

Sophie bit her lip, fighting the urge to scream.

Max's hands shook.

"Did anyone else hear that?" Sarah whispered.

They nodded, eyes wide.

Suddenly, the chandelier overhead swung violently, shattering glass in a sparkling rain.

"RUN!" Jake yelled.

They bolted out of the study, hearts pounding, breaths ragged.

Through twisting corridors, past broken furniture, and past windows showing only darkness, they sprinted.

Behind them, the mansion groaned and whispered, promising it wasn't done yet.

Bursting out the front door, they stumbled onto the overgrown lawn.

The sun was setting, casting long, sinister shadows.

Jake looked back at the mansion, now looming and alive in the dusk.

"We have to come back," Sophie said, voice trembling.

"Come back?" Max said. "Are you crazy? This place almost killed us."

Jake shook his head, eyes burning. "No. We have to come back. We have to find out why it's here... and why it knows us."

Sarah nodded. "Whatever this is, it's just the beginning."

The four stood together, breathless, the jungle closing in behind them—and the haunted mansion waiting silently, hungry for its next move.

II

The Mansion That Doesn't Forget

There's a strange kind of silence that hangs over you after you've nearly been killed by a sentient mirror, chased by a Victorian ghost girl, and possibly had your memories manipulated by a house with bad intentions and creaky floorboards. The kind of silence that isn't peaceful—it's suspicious. And it was exactly that kind of silence now hanging like fog over Jake, Sophie, Max, and Sarah as they trudged through the jungle toward the barely-visible path that might take them back to camp.

"I swear, if a single squirrel jumps out at me, I will cry," Sarah muttered, brushing aside a low-hanging branch that had been sneak-attacking her every five steps.

Jake, still holding the old photograph they'd found in the music box, was unusually quiet. Which meant something was seriously wrong—Jake was only ever quiet when asleep or about to say something stupidly brave.

Sophie, walking beside him, glanced down at the photo again. Four kids. Two girls. Two boys. Same number as them. Similar builds. Similar faces. One boy even had that same annoyingly lopsided smirk Jake always wore when trying to be clever—which was always.

Sophie cleared her throat. "You think this is, like... us?"

Jake didn't answer.

Max, lagging behind them and grumbling with every step, finally burst out: "Okay, look. I know what we saw in that mansion was insane. But ghosts? Possessed mirrors? Creepy music boxes with creepy photos of creepy kids who might be us? I need a reboot. Like—shut me off and turn me back on. I'm done."

"Not to alarm anyone," Sophie said dryly, "but our fearless leader over here hasn't blinked in two minutes."

"I'm fine," Jake muttered. Then tripped over a tree root.

Sarah reached down and helped him up with a smirk. "Smooth."

"Totally did that on purpose," Jake said, brushing dirt off his jeans. "Tactical jungle roll."

"Sure," Max said. "Ten out of ten, very stealthy. Definitely fooled that fern you belly-flopped into."

They finally spotted the flicker of lights through the dense trees—the edges of their school's campsite. Safety. Or at least, relative safety. Because nothing ever feels safe again after a ghost has screamed in your face while hovering upside-down from a ceiling like an angry chandelier.

Back at camp, things felt...off.

Not "possessed-furniture" off, but subtly weird. Their classmates looked at them like they were strangers. Their teacher, Mr. Albright, blinked in confusion when they approached.

"I thought you four were in Cabin 7," he said, frowning. "You were here during headcount."

Sophie squinted. "No, we weren't. We got lost in the jungle. Remember?"

Max added, "You literally told us not to go wandering. We left right after you warned us."

Albright blinked again. "I think you're mistaken. I just saw you guys an hour ago."

Jake's stomach twisted.

Sophie glanced at the others. "That's not right."

Sarah stepped forward. "Wait—are you saying you saw us here? Recently? Like... right now recently?"

Mr. Albright looked annoyed now. "I know you think it's funny to mess with me, but the joke's over. Go get cleaned up."

As he walked away, the four teens stood in silence.

Max broke it with a whisper. "Okay. I'm voting time loop."

Sophie crossed her arms. "No one remembers us being gone?"

Jake looked at his phone. It was exactly the same time as when they'd entered the mansion.

"Okay," he said quietly. "This is officially way past haunted. The mansion's messing with time."

That night in their shared cabin, the unease festered.

The camp was still full of cheerful students, unaware of the eerie house hiding beyond the trees. The group tried to explain what happened to others. No one believed them. No one remembered them being gone.

They might as well have never left.

It was as if time itself had been erased.

"I hate this," Max said, flopping onto his bunk. "I hate time stuff. I hate haunted things. I hate creaking noises. And I swear I heard my backpack whisper my name earlier."

Jake sat on the floor with the photograph spread out in front of him. He turned it over. On the back, faded ink spelled out:

"We were here before. And we'll be here again."

Jake's blood ran cold.

Sophie leaned over his shoulder, reading it aloud. "Creepy much?"

Sarah perched beside him. "It's like... the house is stuck in a cycle. Or maybe we are."

Max was half under his blanket now. "Plot twist: we're all ghosts. Boom."

"Would explain your personality," Jake mumbled.

Max threw a sock at him.

But beneath the jokes, the tension remained.

They couldn't shake it—the feeling that something had followed them out of the mansion.

Around 3 a.m., Jake woke to a sound.

A creak.

The same creak the upstairs hallway in the mansion had made.

He sat up, heartbeat thudding. The room was dark, except for the soft moonlight filtering in through the window. The others were asleep—well, Max was snoring so loud he could be mistaken for summoning a demon.

Another creak.

Jake stood and tiptoed to the window.

Outside, in the tree line, stood a figure.

A girl in a white dress.

The same girl from the mirror.

She lifted a hand and pointed—toward the mansion.

Then she vanished.

Jake didn't tell the others right away. He tried to ignore it. But the image wouldn't leave his mind. The girl. The pointing. The whisper in his ears:

"We're not done."

By the time breakfast rolled around, Jake had bags under his eyes and a serious need for coffee.

Sophie noticed immediately.

"You look like you've aged ten years."

"I feel like I've aged ten years."

Max was too busy pouring cereal into his mouth like a human cement mixer to notice anything. Sarah, though, was already watching Jake carefully.

"Something happened," she said. "What was it?"

Jake leaned in and whispered. "She was outside. The girl from the mirror. Last night."

Max immediately spit cereal across the table.

Sophie slapped her forehead. "Great."

Sarah's voice dropped. "Did she say anything?"

Jake nodded. "She pointed back to the mansion."

There was a pause. Then Max said what they were all thinking:

"Looks like we're going back."

They left at dusk.

Not because it was smart.

Not because it was safe.

But because Jake saw her again—the ghost girl—and this time she didn't just point.

She mouthed something.

"Before it's too late."

So they packed their flashlights, shoved protein bars into their pockets, and snuck out of camp like a group of very attractive idiots with a death wish.

"I'm just saying," Max whispered as they passed the edge of the jungle, "normal teenagers sneak out to party. Or meet someone behind the gym. Not to return to a haunted colonial nightmare with rotting staircases and a ghost who's obviously been watching us sleep."

"Maybe that's what she's into," Jake muttered.

"Don't," Sophie warned. "Don't make the ghost-girl-falls-for-you joke. It's weird. She's dead."

Jake shrugged, walking ahead. "You don't know her story. Maybe she just needs someone emotionally unavailable with great hair."

Sarah laughed softly. "Congratulations. You're officially more unhinged than the door we kicked open last time."

"You're just jealous of my haunted fanbase," Jake said smugly.

Max groaned. "If we die tonight, I want that written on your tombstone. 'Jake: Loved by ghosts. Hated by common sense.'"

The mansion came into view like something that had been waiting for them.

Same towering windows.

Same oppressive roof.

Same feeling of dread curling under their skin like cold fingers.

But tonight, something was different.

It looked... alive.

Soft candlelight glowed in the windows, flickering like the house was hosting a dinner party from the underworld. The door creaked open without them touching it.

"That's not suspicious at all," Sarah whispered.

Sophie nodded grimly. "It knows we're coming."

Max turned to Jake. "I vote we pretend this never happened and tell the camp we went birdwatching."

"Too late," Jake said, stepping forward.

As they crossed the threshold, the temperature dropped instantly. The air turned dense. Almost...wet. Like the walls were breathing.

Sophie shivered. "I swear it's watching us."

Sarah glanced around. "Didn't this entryway look different last time?"

It had.

Where the grand staircase had once been, now stood a corridor of doors—each painted in a different color.

Red. Green. Blue. Yellow.

"Okay," Max said, throwing up his hands. "This isn't how physics works. This isn't even how interior design works."

Jake turned in a slow circle. "The house is changing. Rearranging itself."

"Like a puzzle," Sarah murmured. "Or a test."

They approached the doors.

Each had a symbol etched into it. Jake leaned closer.

The red door had a mirror.

The green one: a heart.

The blue: an eye.

The yellow: a key.

"I'm not touching anything," Max said, backing away. "One of these is going to eat us."

Sophie's fingers hovered over the heart symbol. "What if these are...memories?"

Sarah gave her a sharp look. "Whose?"

Jake's jaw tightened. "Let's find out."

He pushed open the blue door.

Inside was darkness.

Then—

A bright flash.

They stood in a different house now. A kitchen. Warm. Smelling of cinnamon and oranges.

A woman stood at the stove, humming.

And a small boy—Jake—ran past, laughing.

Sophie gasped.

Jake froze. "This is... my childhood home."

The woman turned around.

His mother.

Alive.

Max stepped back, eyes wide. "We're in your memory?"

Jake didn't answer. He was too busy watching.

Young Jake handed a drawing to his mom. She beamed. "Is that our house?"

Jake nodded in the memory. "It's going to be big. With secret rooms."

The memory flickered. Like an old film reel. The scene twisted.

Now the same kitchen—older, colder.

His mother was gone.

Jake sat at the table, older. Silent.

Alone.

Then—

The ghost girl appeared behind him.

Watching.

"I don't remember this," Jake whispered.

The ghost girl turned toward the present-day Jake—and pointed at him.

The scene shattered.

They were yanked out of the room like marionettes, stumbling back into the corridor.

Silence.

Jake's breathing was shallow. "I—I think the house is showing us what we forgot."

Max looked shaken. "Or what it took from us."

Sarah stepped up to the green door, her jaw clenched. "Let's keep going."

They entered her memory.

A ballet studio.

Sarah danced across the floor, graceful, smiling.

Her mom watched proudly through the glass.

Then the scene warped—glass cracking, lights dimming.

Her mom disappeared.

And the studio twisted into the mansion hallway.

A mirror at the far end reflected not Sarah—but the ghost girl in a ballerina's tutu.

Sarah grabbed her head. "I—I know her."

Sophie reached out. "What?"

But before she could answer, the room dissolved again.

One by one, they entered the doors.

Max's memory: A classroom, where he was alone during recess, humming to himself—until a boy appeared and offered him a comic book. That boy? Jake.

"I never remembered that," Max said quietly.

Sophie's memory: A rainy afternoon, a piano recital, nerves in her throat like ice—until another girl joined her on the bench and played alongside her. The girl had long dark hair, soft eyes...

"Sarah?" Sophie whispered.

Sarah nodded slowly. "We've all met before."

Jake's voice was low. "But the house...made us forget."

The yellow door creaked open.

They didn't touch it.

It opened on its own.

Inside: the mansion. Empty. Cold. But different.

In the center: a table. On it, four candles. One for each of them.

And a fifth.

Burning brighter.

"Who's the fifth?" Sophie asked.

The ghost girl stepped forward from the shadows.

Her eyes burned with sorrow.

"I was the fifth."

Then everything went black.

The darkness wasn't silent.

It whispered.

It pulsed.

It breathed.

Each of them stood in a different corner of the void, separated. The air thick like syrup, sounds muffled like underwater screams.

Jake blinked, trying to call out, "Sophie?"

His voice came out distorted. Like it had to travel through an old cassette tape before reaching anyone.

Then—click.

Lights flickered on.

They weren't in the mansion anymore.

They were in a school hallway.

Old. Rusted lockers. Broken tile floors.

And four nameplates glowing faintly on the wall:

JAKE. SOPHIE. MAX. SARAH.

And beneath them—one more name, scrawled in messy cursive:

ADELIA.

Jake stared at it.

The ghost girl had a name.

"Adelia."

Sophie said it aloud as the others appeared beside her, blinking like they'd just crawled out of a dream.

Sarah ran a hand through her hair. "What kind of haunted Scooby-Doo crap is this?"

Max looked genuinely offended. "Why didn't she just tell us her name earlier? Would've saved so much screaming."

"She didn't want to be remembered," Jake said quietly.

Sophie looked at him. "Why not?"

Jake pointed to the lockers.

They were warping.

Bleeding names. Words. Sentences etched in grime.

We played hide and seek.

We left her behind.

She never came back out.

The walls throbbed like a heartbeat. And from behind one locker... a low thud. Then another. Like something—or someone—trapped inside.

Max took a giant step back. "Nope. Nope nope nope."

The locker door flew open.

Adelia.

Not ghostly. Not glowing. Just...a little girl, sitting curled up inside, knees to her chest, eyes wide with fear.

"You left me," she said in a voice no child should ever use.

Sophie knelt down, shaking. "Adelia—we didn't mean to. We don't remember."

"Because the house made you forget," Adelia whispered.

A door opened behind her. The real mansion again.

Adelia stepped out of the locker. Her feet didn't touch the ground.

She floated ahead, not looking back. "Come. It's time."

They followed.

The house groaned.

Candles lit up hallways on their own. Paintings blinked. Carpets slithered like snakes underfoot.

"I hate this place," Max muttered, hopping over a weirdly giggling rug.

Sophie stuck close to Jake. Her shoulder brushed his.

"I'm...scared," she admitted, her voice soft.

Jake gave a dry laugh. "You think I'm not? But hey—if we die, at least it'll be in a historically significant building."

She rolled her eyes but smiled. Then—quietly—she reached out and grabbed his hand.

Jake blinked.

Looked down.

Didn't pull away.

Their fingers laced together.

Sarah and Max both turned to look and immediately groaned in unison.

"Seriously?" Max said. "Romantic hand-holding while the house is clearly vomiting blood on the ceiling?"

Sarah added, "Let's wait until after we survive the demon architecture before we schedule your honeymoon."

Jake gave them a smug smirk. "Jealous?"

Max pointed at a painting that just bled from its eyes. "Of that? Never."

They entered the main ballroom.

At its center: a strange black pillar, covered in names—like a war memorial made of shadow.

Adelia floated to the base and pointed. "There. Look."

The four teens stepped closer.

Their names were carved into the pillar.

And below them—dates.

The same date.

Ten years ago.

"Wait—what?" Sophie whispered. "That's not possible."

"We were...seven," Sarah said slowly. "We weren't even friends back then."

"Wrong," Adelia said. "You were."

She waved a hand.

The ballroom shifted.

They stood in it again—but smaller. Younger. Laughing.

Little Max climbed onto a chair, yelling, "I'm the vampire king!"

Little Sophie and Little Sarah chased him, squealing.

Little Jake? He held hands with a girl in a red ribbon.

Adelia.

She turned to them. "We all came here. Once. On another school trip."

"You went in to play," she whispered. "You told me to hide. Said you'd find me. But you...never came back."

The room darkened.

Little Adelia faded away.

"I died waiting," she said.

The ghostly version of her returned. Older. Eyes glowing.

"And the mansion...fed on it."

Jake stepped forward. "Why erase our memories?"

"Because pain makes the house stronger," she said simply. "If you remembered, you might leave. But forgetting? That keeps you trapped. Keeps the fear fresh."

Max stared at the pillar. "Then why show us this now?"

"Because," Adelia said, her eyes locking onto Sophie. "You're getting closer to remembering everything."

Sophie blinked. "What does that mean?"

Adelia looked down. "You were the one who left me."

Sophie staggered.

"No—I—I couldn't—"

Jake stepped in. "She didn't mean to."

Adelia's face cracked. "She promised. She said she'd come back."

Suddenly, the ballroom split in half.

Cracks tore across the floor.

Wind howled from the broken windows.

And the house began to scream.

"We need to get out!" Sarah shouted.

"No!" Sophie yelled. "We can't leave her again!"

Adelia hovered above them now, glowing like a storm. Her voice echoed in every wall.

"Then play one last game."

The floor vanished.

They fell—

THUD.

They hit the ground.

But it was soft—too soft. Like a giant marshmallow carpet.

"Where...are we?" Sarah groaned, her legs tangled in Max's.

Max blinked. "Are we in—someone's grandma's attic?"

They were in a narrow, musty hallway lit by flickering chandeliers. Everything was covered in floral wallpaper that looked like it hadn't seen sunlight since the Titanic sank. Portraits of faceless people lined the walls. Some moved when they weren't looking.

"Why does this place look like it smells like soup?" Max muttered.

Jake helped Sophie up, brushing cobwebs from her hair. She looked around, pale.

"I think we're...somewhere deeper in the house," she said. "This isn't just haunted. This is...personal."

The hallway creaked.

They turned a corner.

And ended up where they started.

Same chandelier. Same portraits. Same hideous wallpaper.

"No," Sarah said flatly. "Nope. No way. We just walked in a circle."

Jake tested it again. Turned left, then right, then another left—

Same place.

The hallway was looping.

Max knocked on a wall. "Is this...a ghost version of IKEA? Are we stuck in a cursed showroom with no exits?"

Then, all at once, the hallway shifted.

The walls stretched, becoming elastic.

Doors opened where there weren't doors before. One whispered. One moaned. One had teeth.

"Okay, that one's alive," Jake said, yanking Sophie back as the door tried to bite her.

Sarah cursed. "What do we do?!"

Sophie turned to Jake. "We pick a door."

Jake raised a brow. "Randomly?"

"No. Together."

She reached out her hand.

He took it.

Max clutched Sarah's arm. "In case we die, just know—I always thought you were my second favorite after Sophie."

"Aw," Sarah said sarcastically. "Touching. Get eaten first."

They opened the third door.

Behind it was...a field?

Not just any field—a sunlit, warm, golden meadow. Birds chirped. The smell of lavender filled the air.

They blinked at it.

"I...what?" Jake stepped in cautiously.

And then something hit him.

A memory.

Laughter.

Running through the field as a kid.

Sophie by his side. Max tripping over his shoelaces. Sarah doing cartwheels.

Adelia.

Standing by the tree.

She waved at them, smiling.

Then the tree's bark twisted. The sky cracked. The sun bled.

And the field vanished.

Just for a second.

Then it came back.

But now...something was off.

Max pointed at the birds. "Dude. Look at their faces."

The birds had human eyes.

Jake turned slowly. "Okay. Out. We're out."

They ran—straight back through the door.

Back in the hallway.

Now...every door had a symbol.

A bleeding clock. An eye. A broken heart. A star.

Jake's voice was dry. "Let me guess: Choose your trauma?"

Max muttered, "I pick none of the above."

But Sophie was staring at the broken heart.

"It's trying to make us remember things," she whispered. "Good memories. Bad ones. Things it made us forget."

Jake followed her gaze. "That's why it's glitching. We're breaking through the lie."

She looked up at him.

Their eyes locked.

Everything slowed.

The house held its breath.

"I remember," she whispered.

Jake's heart skipped.

"Sophie—what do you—?"

She leaned in.

And she kissed him.

It wasn't slow.

It was urgent, messy, desperate—like they'd waited a decade and just remembered why.

Jake's hands found her waist. Hers tangled in his hoodie.

Max and Sarah both turned around in horror.

"Oh my God," Max gagged. "There are ghosts watching, you guys!"

"Get a coffin, why don't you?" Sarah added.

But then—snap.

The hallway reset.

The door symbols vanished.

The chandeliers reversed their flickering.

Jake and Sophie pulled apart, blinking.

"What were we doing?" Jake asked, confused.

Sophie looked stunned. "I...don't know."

The kiss was gone.

Time loop.

"You've got to be kidding me," Sarah said. "We're in a romantic horror movie directed by a drunk time traveler."

Max looked around. "Hey...where's Adelia?"

Jake turned.

And there she was.

Sitting cross-legged on the ceiling like a spider. Her head twisted 180 degrees to look at them.

"You broke the loop," she said. "Good."

Jake blinked. "We what?"

She dropped to the floor like gravity didn't matter. "Every time you remembered something real, the mansion weakened. Every kiss, every memory, every piece of truth—it hurts it."

Max blinked. "So...we need to keep kissing?"

Sarah turned slowly. "Don't even."

Adelia hovered between two doors now. "You need to reach the core of the house. Where the lies started."

Sophie whispered, "What happens if we fail?"

Adelia's face turned monstrous. Cracked. Old.

"Then the house erases you again. And again. And again."

She floated backwards.

And vanished.

Jake turned to the others.

"We're going."

Sarah raised a brow. "You sure? What if she's messing with us again?"

Jake looked at Sophie. She stared back.

"I don't know," he admitted. "But I remember this much—we left her behind once. We're not doing it again."

Sophie squeezed his hand.

Sarah rolled her eyes. "Fine. Let's go get haunted to death. Again."

Max pulled out his phone. "Signal still dead. But the selfie camera works. Smile for one last photo?"

Jake smirked. "Only if we survive."

Max clicked the button.

FLASH.

In the background of the photo:

Adelia stood smiling between them.

But none of them noticed.

The hallway went silent.

No creaks. No whispers. No ghost-birds. Just an awful, unnatural silence.

Max shifted uncomfortably. "I'd rather the walls scream again. This quiet? Way creepier."

Jake led them forward. The floor felt...different.

Almost like they were walking on water. Or memories.

Sophie looked down.

Images shimmered under their feet.

Snapshots—blurry and disjointed.

Them as kids.

Running. Screaming. Laughing.

A birthday cake.

Max with cake on his face.

Sarah hiding under a table.

Adelia—right in the middle of them.

She looked alive. Happy.

Then her image blinked—her smile distorted.

And suddenly, they remembered.

Ten years ago.

A school trip.

A forest trail.

They'd gotten lost—just like now.

Only back then, it was five of them. Jake, Sophie, Max, Sarah...

And Adelia.

The mansion had found them before.

But only four returned.

And none remembered her after.

The teachers said they'd hallucinated. That Adelia was an "imaginary friend." A made-up game.

But she was real.

The mansion had erased her.

Erased their memories.

Until now.

Jake stumbled. "Oh my God. We left her."

Sophie was shaking. "No. The house took her."

Max's face went pale. "That's why everything's happening again. We came back. The house is...trying to finish the story."

Sarah whispered, "She's trapped in the mansion's core."

A door appeared.

Ancient. Black. Covered in symbols that seemed to breathe.

Jake stepped forward.

"Only one way to find her."

He reached for the knob.

It turned by itself.

Inside was the Memory Room.

An enormous circular chamber, walls made of mirrors and fog. Floating objects from the past drifted mid-air—old toys, a torn backpack, a school permission slip with five names. One crossed out: Adelia Gray.

The room pulsed like a heartbeat.

Adelia stood at its center.

Except...not the child version.

She was older now.

Same age as them.

But...strange. Her eyes glowed faintly. Her hair floated like she was underwater.

"Adelia?" Sophie whispered.

Adelia turned.

And smiled.

But it was wrong.

"You came back," she said softly. "I waited so long."

Jake stepped forward. "We didn't remember. The house made us forget."

Adelia's voice wavered. "I know. I screamed every night, hoping one of you would hear me. But you forgot. You all left me."

Max opened his mouth. "We didn't mean to—"

"I know," she said, her voice cracking. "But the mansion...it got lonely. So it kept me. And then it became me."

Her skin rippled. Shadow and flame flickered beneath it.

The mansion had made her its heart.

Jake felt a weight in his chest. "Adelia...we're here now. Let us take you home."

She shook her head, eyes glassy.

"I can't leave. Not unless someone stays in my place."

The walls groaned.

The deal had been made.

Sarah glared. "No way. There has to be another way."

Adelia blinked tears. "I don't want any of you to stay. I just want it to end."

The mirrors cracked.

The fog thickened.

Sophie took Jake's hand. "What do we do?"

Max pulled out the school permission slip. "Look at this! This proves she existed! This proves we weren't crazy!"

The slip burst into flame in his hands.

The mansion rejected it.

Adelia's voice echoed—two voices layered. Hers and the house's.

"Only one trade. Only one path."

Jake stepped forward.

"No," Sophie said, gripping his arm.

But Jake turned, his eyes soft.

"I'll do it. I'm the one who kept feeling something was wrong. I knew it all along. Let me make it right."

"NO," she snapped. "You're not dying for me, Jake!"

"I'm not dying," he said with a sad smile. "Just...remember me this time."

The room quaked.

Adelia reached toward Jake, but suddenly—

Max pulled him back.

"Enough of this guilt-sacrifice crap!" he shouted. "No one's staying!"

Sarah raised her fists. "We're four idiots, remember? We fight. We flirt. We scream like children. But we don't LEAVE anyone behind!"

They all locked hands.

And something changed.

The mirrors exploded outward.

The fog peeled back.

The mansion screamed.

Not in anger.

In pain.

Adelia fell to her knees.

The room started collapsing.

The spell was breaking.
Jake reached for her.
And this time—
She took his hand.
Everything went white.
And then—
They were standing in the forest.
Back in daylight.
The mansion?
Gone.
No trace.
No fog. No vines. No howling ghosts.
Just trees and birds.
Adelia stood beside them—alive. Whole. Shaking.
They turned to one another.
They remembered everything.
They walked until they found the search team, who had apparently been looking for them for days, not hours. Time worked differently in the mansion.
When they tried to explain...
Nobody believed them.
The story made no sense.
The mansion didn't exist on any map.
And the school denied any record of "Adelia Gray."
That night, Max sat on his bed, flipping through photos on his phone.
He stopped on the selfie they took before entering the Memory Room.
There she was.
Adelia.
Clear as day.
Smiling behind them.

III

Midnight Games and Dead Things in the Walls

There's something deeply unsettling about a school at night. The way the walls hum like they're breathing. The flickering hallway lights. The silence that feels too thick, like it's listening. Jake had never believed the haunted school stories—until now.

And now, standing just outside the main hallway of Crestwood High, he was beginning to feel like they'd walked out of a nightmare only to fall into another.

The school should've been safe. Familiar. But it wasn't.

Sophie clung to his arm, eyes wide. Her breath came in shallow gasps, and Jake could feel the tremble in her grip. Sarah and Max stood behind them, equally frozen. And then there was Adelia—silent, pale, staring down the corridor like she was seeing ghosts.

Because she was.

At the far end of the hallway, students were filing out of their classrooms. Only, they weren't... normal. They moved too slowly, arms hanging limp, faces blank. Their eyes glowed faintly in the dim light, white and lifeless. No one spoke. No one blinked. It was like the entire student body had been turned into sleepwalking zombies.

Max whispered, "Okay, plot twist: the haunted mansion followed us home."

Jake swallowed hard. "They're heading for the basement."

"That's where we go away from," Sarah hissed. "Away from the spooky dimension. Not toward it like some horror movie extras asking to die."

But Adelia spoke then, her voice low and distant. "It's not them. Not anymore. The mansion... it found a crack. A way out."

Sophie shook her head. "No. No, no. We left it behind. We broke the spell, right? That was the point of nearly dying six times and throwing holy water on a possessed toilet."

Adelia turned slowly, her eyes glistening with tears. "You didn't free me. You opened something. And now it's seeping through."

The door to the basement groaned open before them. Not the rusted, always-locked one they'd seen for years. This one was black wood. Ornate carvings. Old. Ancient. Wrong. It didn't belong in any modern building, let alone a high school.

Jake took a slow step forward.

"Don't you dare," Sophie said, grabbing his hoodie like a lifeline.

"I have to check," he said, his voice steady. "If we wait too long, those kids... whatever's down there could finish what the mansion started."

"Or it could finish you," she said, eyes narrowed. "Don't you dare sacrifice yourself like some dramatic horror protagonist with a death wish."

Jake turned and gave her a small grin. "Not planning on dying. Yet."

Sarah glanced at Max. "We going with him?"

Max groaned. "I swear, if I die, I'm haunting your laundry room forever."

They followed.

The basement stairs were not stairs anymore. The first three steps looked normal. Concrete, stained with mop water and chalk dust. But the fourth step shimmered. Shifted. And turned into wood. The fifth groaned like a coffin lid. The sixth hissed.

By the seventh, the air changed.

Jake felt it in his lungs.

The cold, choking pressure.

They weren't in the school anymore.

The mansion was back.

Or worse—the school had become the mansion.

The hallway at the bottom stretched longer than it should've. Doors lined the walls, some open, revealing shifting rooms inside—classrooms morphing into grand libraries with floating books, bathrooms turning into candlelit corridors. The building was folding into itself. Warping.

Max pointed at a locker that was bleeding.

"Okay, if my hallucination is also seeing this, we're screwed."

They moved carefully, stepping over cracks in the floor that breathed like mouths. Occasionally, a voice would whisper from nowhere. Names. Secrets. Sarah paused when she heard her own name spoken in her mother's voice. Sophie turned white when she heard someone whisper Jake's name like a lover.

"This place knows too much," she muttered.

Adelia guided them forward.

At the end of the corridor, a door stood waiting. Black and tall, pulsing faintly like a heartbeat. Carved across it were the words: Final Game Begins.

Jake touched the knob.

It burned.

He pulled back, hissing.

"Wait," Sarah said. "Game? What game?"

Adelia's expression twisted. "The mansion's magic is ancient. Old spirits, old power. It runs on rituals. Rules. It wants us to play."

Max exhaled. "Great. Creepy demonic Monopoly."

"No," Adelia whispered. "It's something older. More dangerous. A memory game. It wants to feed."

Jake looked back at them. "We go in together. No one splits up. We end this."

They nodded.

He opened the door.

What lay beyond made every cell in their bodies scream.

It was the Memory Room again—but bigger now. Stretching forever. Mirrors covered every surface—ceiling, floor, walls—each one reflecting not just their current selves, but versions of them. Children. Teenagers. Elderly. Dead.

Sophie looked into one and gasped.

It showed her standing in the mansion's foyer, but this version of her was... different. Paler. Colder. And she was holding something.

A knife.

Covered in blood.

"I don't like this," she whispered. "This isn't me."

Jake stared into a mirror that showed him burning. Another one where he was crying over a grave. Another where he was kissing Sophie—and then vanishing into dust.

Max, meanwhile, found one where he was being chewed on by a clown with antlers. He screamed and kicked the glass.

"Okay, that's enough of that."

But none of the mirrors cracked.

They absorbed the blows. And they began to whisper. Softly at first. Then louder.

"You don't belong here."

"You've seen too much."

"You are already ours."

Jake spun. "We need to find the core. The heart of this place. Before it finds us."

Suddenly, one of the mirrors cracked.

Then another.

Then all of them.

The room filled with laughter.

And a shadow stepped out from the far end.

It was... Jake.

Another Jake.

But taller, more elegant, dressed like a Victorian prince. His eyes glowed gold.

"Finally," he said. "The real game begins."

IV

The Hallway That Shouldn't Exist

Jake couldn't breathe. For a moment, it was as if reality had folded in on itself—school walls that weren't supposed to exist pressing in from every side. The library's silence was deafening, the fluorescent lights buzzing like an awkward pause in conversation. It was too bright. Too clean. Too normal.

And that was the most terrifying part.

Max sat criss-cross on the carpet, rubbing his face like he'd just been hit by a truck. "So... we're just back now? Like—bam, horror over, back to our regularly scheduled math tests?"

Sarah was staring out the glass-paneled window. "Something's wrong."

"You think?" Sophie replied, crossing her arms. "We were just talking to ghost kids that looked exactly like us."

"No, not that," Sarah said quietly. "Look."

Outside, the school courtyard was empty. No students. No teachers. Just... fog. Thick, rolling fog swallowing the world beyond the glass. Trees that shouldn't have been there—crooked, warped, their bark looking almost like faces screaming mid-silent agony—circled the building like a barrier.

Jake's chest tightened. "This isn't real. We're not back."

"We're in a copy of the school," Sophie murmured. "The mansion made it."

"A cursed IKEA showroom version," Max added helpfully. "Y'know, just in case we needed a fake library to get haunted in."

Jake stepped away from the group, trying to listen past the buzzing lights. There—beneath the hum. A heartbeat. Slow. Wet. Almost mechanical.

He turned toward the double doors that led out of the library. They were cracked open. Just enough to tempt.

Sarah looked at them nervously. "Did we come in that way?"

"Nope," said Max. "I would've remembered the infinite horror vibes."

Jake walked over and nudged the door open farther.

Behind it...

A hallway.

But not the school hallway.

This one stretched on forever. The walls were covered in faded floral wallpaper that peeled in long, curling strips. The floor was damp. Wooden. Old. And the ceiling?

The ceiling dripped.

Sophie moved to Jake's side, brushing his shoulder with hers. "We're not done, are we?"

"Nope."

Max, with his usual theatrical flair, groaned. "Why is it always hallways? Can't we just teleport into a Chili's for once?"

They stepped into the hallway.

Instantly, the temperature dropped. Their breath clouded in front of them. The door behind them slammed shut with a sound that echoed like a gunshot. They jumped.

"Well, now we're trapped," Sarah said flatly. "Again."

Jake led the way, stepping carefully over broken floorboards. Shadows danced ahead of them. The walls creaked and sighed, like the house was dreaming around them.

Then a voice whispered from behind the wallpaper: "You left us here..."

They froze.

Sophie's hand found Jake's.

"Keep walking," Jake whispered.

Footsteps echoed up ahead.

Someone—or something—was walking just beyond the curve in the hallway. A child's giggle floated toward them, followed by the soft shuffle of bare feet on wood.

Max whispered, "If it's a kid, I swear I'm gonna throw it out the window. Ghost or not."

They turned the corner—

And saw a little girl standing under a dim ceiling bulb, back turned to them, her long hair hiding her face.

The bulb above her flickered once, twice—

She turned slowly.

No eyes.

Just two gaping holes, leaking black tears down her cheeks.

She smiled.

Jake took a step back.

The girl opened her mouth and screamed—not with sound, but with light. A blinding flash burst from her mouth and the walls around them shifted, peeling away like skin. The hallway blinked—and became something else.

Now they stood in a massive ballroom.

The ceiling stretched impossibly high. Chandeliers hung like frozen screams, cracked and swaying. The floor was marble, but rotting. Tables with untouched feasts sat in decayed glory. Everything was beautiful—and dead.

A waltz began playing from somewhere. A piano with no player.

Then... couples appeared.

Dancing.

Elegant. Dressed in Victorian gowns and suits. But faceless.

Their heads were smooth ovals of skin.

Max took one look and muttered, "Okay, that's it. I'm done. This is where I die. In a Tim Burton fever dream."

Sophie pointed to the edge of the room. "There. Another hallway. Come on—"

But before they could move, one of the dancers broke off.

And turned toward them.

Its body snapped, bones cracking in reverse, until it moved like a spider on two legs.

Jake raised his fists. "Back up. Slowly."

But the dancer opened its mouth—where its face should've been—and the same blinding light poured out.

Boom.

Another shift.

They fell again—this time into darkness.

Jake hit the ground hard, the breath punched out of him.

Stone floor.

Damp. Cold. Smelled like mold, copper, and the bitter tang of something ancient.

"Everyone okay?" he wheezed, blinking in the pitch black.

"Define okay," Max grumbled, somewhere to his left. "Because I just kissed a slab of stone harder than I've ever kissed a girl."

"Same," Sophie muttered. "Except I think the stone kissed back."

Sarah groaned. "Where are we now?"

Jake's hand fumbled for his phone. He clicked on the flashlight.

The small beam of light sliced through the black.

They were in a tunnel.

A narrow, curved, stone tunnel—arched like an ancient crypt. Moss grew in thick patches along the walls. Water dripped somewhere in the distance. And every surface was covered in carvings.

Not just symbols. Faces.

Hundreds of them.

Some with mouths open in eternal screams. Others with hollow sockets where eyes should've been.

"Did we just fall through the haunted version of Google Maps?" Max muttered, peering at the grotesque wall decor. "Because this is like, ten stars on the 'nope' scale."

Sophie brushed her fingers over one of the carved faces. "This one... this one looks like..."

She trailed off.

Jake turned his light.

And froze.

The face was hers.

Or at least, close enough. Softer. Younger. Like Sophie when she was maybe ten years old.

Sarah stepped forward and pointed at another face. "That one's me."

"And that one—" Jake's light moved—"is me."

They weren't just carvings.

They were memories.

Locked in stone.

"Wait," Max said slowly. "If we were here before... and we don't remember..."

"The mansion took it from us," Jake said, his voice low. "It erased everything."

Sophie's eyes narrowed. "But why?"

No one had an answer.

They kept walking, each step squelching on the wet stone. The tunnel curved, sloped downward, then upward again, until finally it opened into a circular chamber.

A giant mirror stood in the center.

Cracked.

Fractured in a hundred different places—but somehow still whole.

The mirror shimmered—not with their reflections—but with versions of them.

Sophie gasped.

Inside the glass, she saw herself laughing. Happy. Holding hands with Jake. A picnic. A summer day. A memory that didn't exist—but felt real.

Jake stepped forward.

In his reflection, he was fighting something. Screaming Sophie's name. Covered in blood. Max and Sarah were behind him, younger, terrified.

Sarah stared, eyes wide. "These aren't mirrors. They're memories."

"Or futures," Max said. "Or both."

Jake's reflection turned and stared at him.

And whispered.

Jake stumbled back. "It said—'You failed her again.'"

Sophie's hand gripped his. "Who? Who did you fail?"

"I don't know."

But in the pit of his stomach, something twisted. He did know. Somewhere deep down.

The mirror cracked louder.

A web of glowing red spread across its surface.

"Guys," Max said. "I think we should leave."

Too late.

The glass exploded outward.

A torrent of black smoke poured from the shards, coiling like serpents. The room spun. The faces on the wall screamed—loud, shrieking, and alive.

Jake grabbed Sophie. Max and Sarah huddled together as the smoke circled them.

From within the fog, a voice boomed.

"You broke the rules..."

Sarah shouted over the roar. "What rules?!"

"You remembered."

The fog slammed into them like a tidal wave.

Jake didn't black out this time.

No—this time, the mansion wanted him awake.

Wide awake.

He opened his eyes and found himself standing alone. A pale spotlight above him flickered, casting long, jagged shadows across the floor.

Stone again.

But this time, the stone bled.

Thin rivulets of red trickled along the cracks, pulsing faintly, like veins in a dying beast.

"Sophie?" he called out.

His voice echoed—too many times. As if it was being repeated by something just out of view. Something that was listening. Imitating.

"Sophie..."

"...ophie..."

"...ie..."

A whisper close to his ear.

Jake spun around. No one.

He started walking.

The hallway twisted with every step. Sometimes wider. Sometimes impossibly narrow, forcing him to sidestep along the wall. The air grew warmer—almost humid. Like the mansion was breathing.

And then he heard it.

Laughter.

Children's laughter.

He turned a corner—and froze.

Four kids sat on the floor of a room covered in crayon drawings. The drawings were chaotic—stick figures, strange symbols, blood-red suns, and what looked like... the mansion itself.

The kids looked about eight or nine.

One of them looked exactly like Max.

Another—Jake's breath hitched—was a young version of himself. Sitting next to a girl who looked like Sophie, grinning as she smeared red crayon across the paper like it was finger paint.

The fourth kid had Sarah's eyes.

Jake staggered forward, trying to understand. "We were here..."

He remembered, just for a second.

A secret clubhouse.

A dare.

A door that only opened when you didn't look at it.

Then it was gone.

The ghost children looked up at him in unison.

"You forgot us," said Mini-Sarah.

"You left," said Mini-Sophie.

"You broke it," said Mini-Max.

"You lied," whispered Mini-Jake, his smile curling into something sharp.

Jake backed away.

"Where are the others? Where's Sophie?"

"You can't protect her," they said together. "Not again."

The room rippled.

The children's faces twisted. Melted. Bones cracked. Eyes bled.

Jake turned and ran.

The hallway warped behind him, stretching like rubber. Doors slammed shut as he passed them. He turned another corner—

And collided with Sophie.

Both of them tumbled to the ground.

"Jake?!" she gasped, her face pale. "You okay?"

He pulled her into a hug without thinking. "You're here. Thank god."

Her arms wrapped around him tightly, and for one shaky second, the world stilled.

Then Max and Sarah appeared, stumbling out of a different hallway.

"Don't go into the nursery," Max said immediately, pale as chalk. "It's full of dolls. Like, a billion of them. One winked at me."

Sarah smacked him. "We almost got eaten!"

"By a cradle," Max added. "Not exaggerating. A literal possessed baby bed."

Jake stood up, his heart still racing. "We saw something too. Us. But... younger."

"We've all been here before," Sarah said. "I'm sure of it now."

Sophie nodded. "But why don't we remember?"

The air shifted.

The hallway behind them opened slowly, revealing a spiral staircase that descended into blackness.

"Looks like that's our next stop," Jake said grimly.

Max groaned. "Stairs. Great. Can't wait to fall down and break my personality."

As they stepped onto the first stair, a faint ticking began.

A grandfather clock, hidden somewhere far below, keeping time in a house that shouldn't exist.

The walls whispered as they descended.

"Tick, tock…"

The staircase didn't end.

It just kept going.

Every twist downward made the air heavier, like they were sinking into the mansion's lungs. The walls were no longer stone—they became a mash of flesh-like textures and squishy carpet, sometimes cold marble, sometimes warm wood that pulsed under their feet like it had a heartbeat.

Jake gripped the railing, half-expecting it to turn into a snake.

Max was mumbling behind him. "This is like an Escher painting made by Satan. I swear if a goat with six eyes shows up playing the violin, I'm quitting life."

"I'd pay to see that," Sarah said dryly.

Sophie was quiet.

Jake noticed. She hadn't said much since they reunited. He slowed a little to walk beside her.

"You okay?" he asked.

Sophie didn't answer right away.

Then, softly, "Back in that hallway… I saw something. Me. You. The others. It felt like a memory, but it wasn't. Not exactly."

Jake hesitated. "Me too."

She looked at him, expression guarded. "Do you think we… used to know each other?"

He looked away. "I feel like I've known you forever."

"Funny," she said, a tiny smile playing at her lips. "You don't seem like the sentimental type."

Jake chuckled. "That's because I bury everything under sarcasm and dumb courage."

Sophie bumped his shoulder. "Well, it's kind of working."

Their moment was shattered when Max screamed.

They whipped around—just in time to see Max tumble through what looked like a sheer veil of shadow.

Sarah gasped. "MAX!"

They rushed down—Jake led the charge—straight through the veil.

Suddenly they weren't on stairs anymore.

They were in a massive underground hall. Gothic arches, long faded red carpet, and massive stained-glass windows on either side—though there was no outside, just more mansion stretching into infinite blackness beyond the panes.

Max was sitting in the middle of the carpet, rubbing his head.

Jake sighed in relief. "You good?"

"No. I landed on my sarcasm gland."

Sophie helped Sarah down the last step. "Where are we?"

They all turned slowly.

At the far end of the hall stood a stage.

And on the stage... four chairs.

Each labeled.

Jake. Sophie. Max. Sarah.

Jake stepped forward slowly. "This is starting to feel like one big setup."

"Or therapy," Sarah muttered. "Really bad therapy."

When they approached the stage, something clicked behind them.

Doors slammed.

A spotlight flared to life over the chairs.

And a voice boomed from nowhere, everywhere:

"Choose your seat. Confess your truth. Or stay in the house forever."

Max blinked. "Well, that escalated."

Jake exchanged looks with the others.

Then walked to his chair. "We do this together."

One by one, they followed.

As soon as they sat, metal bands locked around their wrists and ankles.

Max: "I take back my 'we do this together' agreement. I vote to do this not together."

Sophie rolled her eyes. "Too late now."

The room darkened.

And a new figure emerged on the stage—wearing a mask. Tall. Pale suit. No voice.

It held a mirror and walked to Jake first.

A scene appeared in the glass.

Jake, younger, standing outside the mansion's gates. Crying. Alone.

"No," Jake whispered. "No, no, no—"

The voice returned. "Confess, Jake."

He gritted his teeth. "I... I remembered. I knew we'd been here before. But I kept quiet. Because I was scared."

The mirror shimmered.

The shackles on his wrist clicked open.

Sophie looked at him, stunned. "You knew?"

Jake nodded once, ashamed. "Just pieces. But enough."

The masked figure moved to Sophie.

Another image. A letter. Burned.

Sophie stared, tears pricking her eyes. "It was from you. From... back then. I found it when I was twelve. But I thought I made it up. A dream. So I burned it."

"Confess."

Sophie's voice cracked. "I didn't want to believe I'd forgotten people I loved."

Her shackles unlocked.

The masked figure moved on.

Max's turn.

The mirror showed him laughing, pushing Jake, slamming the mansion door closed from the inside.

Max blanched. "I... I dared us to go in. That first time. I wanted to prove I wasn't a coward. Even if it got us all trapped."

The chains fell from him.

Sarah's turn.

The mirror showed her whispering into a crack in the wall—then the door opening.

She looked pale. "I was the one who found the chant. I read it out loud. I opened the mansion."

She didn't cry—but her hands were shaking.

"Confess," the voice said.

"I wanted to belong. I thought if I did something big, you'd all like me more. I didn't know it would... ruin everything."

Her cuffs snapped open.

The lights dimmed.

The masked figure bowed—and vanished.

The stage disappeared beneath their feet.

They fell—again.

But this time, they landed somewhere warmer.

A soft bedroom.

Books. A fire. Clean air.

Sophie looked around in awe. "Is this... safe?"

Jake nodded slowly. "Maybe the mansion gave us a break."

Max flopped onto a velvet couch. "You'd think after emotionally gutting us, it would at least serve pizza."

Jake sat beside Sophie.

She leaned her head against his shoulder.

Quietly, she said, "I'm glad I remembered. Even if it hurts."

He nodded. "Same."

Max, lying across Sarah's lap now like a lazy cat, smirked. "Well, look at that. Haunted mansion therapy works."

Sarah rolled her eyes. "Idiot."

But she didn't push him off.

The strange comfort of the velvet room didn't last.

The fire in the fireplace began to flicker blue.

The shadows lengthened—twisting not with the flames, but against them.

Sophie sat upright, tense. "Something's wrong."

Max groaned. "Can't we have five minutes without the house trying to eat us?"

Jake stood up, scanning the room. "It feels… fake. Like a dream trying too hard to look normal."

Sarah moved to the window. "There's no outside. Just fog."

Jake walked over. "Maybe it's a memory. A trap dressed as comfort."

"Like psychological bubble wrap," Max added. "Smells nice, then kills you."

Sophie pulled open a wardrobe near the bed. Inside: four school backpacks.

Hers.

Jake's.

Max's.

Sarah's.

Exactly as they'd had them when they got lost in the jungle. Exactly how they remembered them.

Even the little Sharpie heart Sophie had drawn on Jake's zipper.

Jake stared. "These weren't with us. We lost them in the forest…"

Sarah's voice was barely a whisper. "The house is putting things back."

Then the bed creaked.

They all turned.

There was someone lying under the blanket.

No one had noticed them before.

The blanket rose and fell with breathing.

Max swore. "Nope. Nope. Not doing this again."

Jake motioned them back and slowly reached for the blanket corner.

He pulled.

Beneath the blanket was…

Jake.

Or a version of him—paler, bruised, with eyes wide open and completely black.

The clone Jake grabbed his wrist.

"You can't leave until it ends again."

Jake yanked free and staggered back.

The lights shattered.

The fireplace hissed.

And the walls began to bleed.

No more pretending. No more warmth.

The mansion was awake.

It had given them a moment of peace—just to watch it burn.

They ran.

Doors appeared and vanished as they sprinted through twisting corridors that shouldn't exist. Hallways moved like conveyor belts. Pictures screamed. The floor tried to devour their feet. And the entire time, they heard that same ticking—faster, louder.

Tick. Tock. Tick. Tock.

They turned a corner—and saw it.

A door they hadn't seen before.

Different.

Gold-lined. Carved with the four of them as children. Their real names etched above: Jake, Sophie, Max, Sarah.

Jake reached for the handle.

It was warm.

He opened it.

Inside: a dining hall. Long table. Dozens of candles.

And sitting at the head—

An old woman. Tall, thin, her skin like cracked paper. Dressed in mourning black. A grin stretched too wide across her face.

"Welcome back, my darlings," she crooned.

Max whispered, "I don't like her smile. I don't like anything about her."

The woman stood, arms spread like a host welcoming guests.

"You finally returned. I've kept your seats warm."

Sophie took a step forward. "Who... are you?"

The woman tilted her head. "Why, I'm your hostess. Your guide. Your judge. And... your grandmother."

Sarah blinked. "Excuse me—what?!"

Jake stepped forward. "That's not possible. None of us—"

"Remember?" she said gently. "Of course you don't. That's how the house works. It feeds on memory. On emotion. On forgotten guilt."

The candles flickered higher.

"You've all been here before. And you left a part of yourselves behind. I simply... kept them safe."

The shadows around the room shimmered—and four shadowy duplicates stepped forward behind her. Copies of the teens—dead-eyed, emotionless.

"Now," the woman whispered, "it's time to put you back together."

The room went cold.

The teens looked at each other.

Sophie's voice was trembling. "We can't let her win. No matter what."

Jake nodded. "We stay together. No running. No more secrets."

Max cracked his knuckles. "I vote we light the table on fire and run screaming."

Sarah rolled her eyes. "And I vote we actually fight back."

The woman grinned wider. "Oh, children..."

"Let the game begin."

And the candles blew out.

V

Dinner With the Dead

The candles had blown out—but somehow, the room wasn't completely dark.

A thin, unnatural glow came from beneath the long dining table, casting eerie shadows upward onto the faces of the four teens.

Jake reached for Sophie's hand in the dark. She didn't hesitate—she gripped his tightly.

"Don't let go," he whispered.

Max edged closer to Sarah, muttering, "If I die, please delete my browser history."

"Noted," Sarah replied dryly, though her hand subtly grabbed the edge of his hoodie sleeve. "You're not dying. Yet."

The old woman—still standing at the head of the table—had not moved since the last candle went out. Her eyes glowed faintly, like coals smoldering in the ash.

"You're not real," Jake said, trying to sound more confident than he felt. "None of this is."

"Oh, child," she whispered, "I'm as real as your guilt. And twice as hungry."

She motioned.

The four shadow-clones of Jake, Sophie, Max, and Sarah stepped forward from behind her, gliding silently around the long table. They moved stiffly, like puppets on invisible strings.

Sophie stared at her double. "That's not just a copy. That's... me."

The clone looked back at her with hollow eyes, then smiled.

Jake grabbed a candlestick from the table and held it like a bat. "I swear if zombie-me tries to bite me, I'm taking him out."

But the clones didn't attack.

Instead, they pulled out the chairs.

Sat down.

And waited.

The old woman clapped her hands once.

Suddenly, the table filled with food.

Steaming roasts. Bowls of fruit. Loaves of bread that looked too perfect. Wine that shimmered black. And a cake taller than Max, decorated with what looked suspiciously like teeth.

Jake's stomach turned.

Max blinked. "Okay. It looks amazing. But there's a high chance that ham is made of despair."

The old woman tilted her head, speaking with sickening sweetness. "You must be starving. All that running and remembering. Sit, my children. Feast."

Sarah leaned closer to Sophie. "You think if we sit, she'll try to trap us?"

Sophie nodded. "Absolutely."

Max had already started pulling out a chair. "Cool. Just checking. I'm starving."

Sarah yanked him back. "Do you ever listen?"

Jake was staring at his clone again. The way it sat—too still, too calm. It didn't breathe. Didn't blink.

He turned to the woman. "What do you want?"

She grinned. "To help you finish what you started."

Jake's heart thudded. "What we started... when?"

She walked around the table, each step quiet as death.

"You all came here once. Many years ago. You were children. Curious. Stupid. Delicious."

She reached Sophie and cupped her chin. Sophie flinched, but didn't pull away.

"You found the room with the mirror. You said the chant. You broke the seal."

Jake felt ice crawl up his spine.

"We were the ones who opened this place?" he asked slowly.

The woman nodded. "Oh, yes. And then, when the house began to feed, when it tasted your guilt, your secrets, your fears... you ran."

She moved to Jake now, her fingers tracing his jaw like a proud mother.

"You tried to leave. And one of you didn't make it."

Silence fell like a hammer.

The woman's eyes gleamed.

"That's why the town forgot. Why your families moved away. Why the forest grew wild. The house needed to be hidden. Because one of you never escaped."

Sophie whispered, "Who?"

The woman shrugged.

"Memory is a fragile thing. Even the house has trouble keeping track."

Jake's voice cracked. "Are you saying one of us is already dead?"

"No, no, no," she purred. "I'm saying one of you is a ghost pretending to be alive."

The four teens went silent.

The four clones watched them, mouths twitching into tiny grins.

Then, suddenly, all at once—the clones began mimicking them.

Sophie's clone reached for Jake's hand. Sarah's clone crossed her legs just like her. Max's clone leaned on the table, smirking in the same lazy way.

And Jake's clone?

It stared at Jake—and mouthed something.

"You died first."

Jake backed up, knocking over his chair.

"No. No, I didn't."

Max looked at him, unsettled. "Bro..."

Jake shook his head. "They're messing with us. Trying to divide us."

The old woman sat at the head of the table again. "You should eat. It may be your last supper."

The teens didn't move.

Then Sophie narrowed her eyes. "This is a test. The confessions, the dinner, the guilt—everything. The house feeds off secrets. But now it's playing mind games."

Sarah nodded slowly. "It wants us to doubt each other. To turn on each other."

Max pulled out a flask from his hoodie pocket. "I have holy water from the chapel room we passed two hours ago. I say we try throwing it on the cake and see what explodes."

Jake looked at him. "You've had holy water this whole time?"

Max shrugged. "You said bring supplies. I brought snacks and divine protection."

Jake snorted, then turned serious. "Okay. We don't eat. We don't play along. We figure out how to break this memory cycle."

The woman tsked. "You're not being very polite, my dears."

Then she raised her hands—and the clones lunged.

Jake barely had time to react.

His clone launched at him, knocking over two chairs as it tackled him to the floor. Cold fingers grabbed at his neck—too strong, too fast. It wasn't just copying him. It was him. Strength, reflexes, even the smirk.

"Get off!" Jake shouted, grappling with his own face.

Sophie screamed as her own doppelgänger sprang across the table like a spider, arms stretched unnaturally wide, nails slicing the tablecloth. Sarah yanked Sophie back just in time and slammed a chair into clone-Sophie's side. It shattered—but the clone didn't even flinch.

Max, meanwhile, was trying to punch himself in the face.

"I knew I'd hate me in a fight!" he shouted, dodging a kick from clone-Max and trying to land one of his own.

Clone-Max laughed. "You hit like a wet sock, bro."

Jake wrestled his double onto the floor, both of them grunting, gritting, and growling. The clone's mouth opened too wide—revealing row after row of jagged, sharklike teeth.

"Okay, that's not part of my dental plan," Jake hissed.

Sophie ducked under the table and grabbed a fork, stabbing it straight into clone-Sophie's hand. It shrieked—a horrible, high-pitched sound that made all four real teens flinch in pain.

"They're connected!" Sophie shouted. "We hurt them—it weakens us!"

Max glanced over, bleeding from his temple. "Then what the hell are we supposed to do—hug them to death?"

Sarah snarled and grabbed the wine goblet near her plate. Without hesitation, she flung its shimmering black liquid into clone-Sarah's face.

The clone stopped moving.

Then it melted.

Straight down into the floor, like a wax figure thrown onto fire.

Sarah's mouth dropped open. "That worked?!"

Jake, hearing that, reached across the table and snatched the same black wine goblet from his clone's seat.

He splashed it across clone-Jake's head.

SIZZLE.

The creature screamed—and collapsed into smoke.

Sophie looked around. "It's the wine! Whatever that black stuff is—it's the key!"

Max grabbed a goblet, spun, and tossed it into clone-Max's chest. "Cheers, ugly!"

Poof. Gone.

Sophie backed up, clone-Sophie approaching like a silent stalker.

No goblet nearby.

No wine.

But she locked eyes with her double.

"You're not me," she whispered. "You're what I used to be. What I was, before I chose to feel something again."

The clone paused.

Hesitated.

Sophie stepped forward. "I'm not afraid of you anymore."

She leaned in—cheek to cheek.

And softly said, "Goodbye."

Clone-Sophie's body began to twitch, spasm—then folded into mist.

Gone.

Jake stared at Sophie like she'd just cast a spell.

"What was that?"

Sophie wiped her hands on her jeans, breathing hard. "Emotional closure. Weirdly effective."

Max raised a hand. "Okay, we need more goth wine and therapy speeches. That's our new weapon."

They didn't have time to celebrate.

The old woman at the head of the table rose again, still smiling—but this time, the smile had cracked. Literally. Her face had begun to split at the corners, deep red lines oozing black.

"You're growing strong," she said. "Too strong."

She raised both arms.

The dining hall began to collapse.

Not explode—collapse.

Walls bending inward. Candles sucked into the void. The table pulled like a spaghetti noodle into a whirlpool of darkness.

Jake grabbed Sophie.

Max caught Sarah's wrist.

"GO!" Jake shouted.

They ran, sprinting across the breaking floorboards, dodging falling debris and phantom hands reaching out of the walls. The hallway they'd entered through had vanished, replaced by an impossible spiral staircase that twisted upward into glowing red mist.

Sophie yelled, "This wasn't here before!"

Max groaned, "I swear if this ends in another library I'm going to throw a bookshelf at someone!"

They climbed.

And climbed.

And climbed.

Every step felt heavier. As if the house was fighting them. Each stair vibrated with whispers. Each landing showed a flicker of old memories—birthday parties, childhood games, a night spent sleeping in tents.

Flash.

A young Jake, blowing out candles.

Flash.

Sophie and Sarah, dressed as witches, holding plastic pumpkins.

Flash.

Max crying in the dark, alone in a hallway.

They reached the top.

A single black door.

Sophie hesitated. "We're not... dead, right?"

Jake shook his head. "No. But the house is trying to rewrite us."

Max touched the door.

It opened.

Beyond: a room made entirely of mirrors.

And inside it—a version of the house they'd never seen before.

It was pristine. Restored. Grand chandeliers. Beautiful furniture. Gold and velvet and marble. The original version of the mansion—before it was corrupted.

And standing in the center: a fifth child.

A boy.

About their age.

Dark-haired, pale, dressed in old-fashioned clothes.

He turned as they entered.

And smiled.

"Took you long enough."

Sophie whispered, "Who... are you?"

He tilted his head. "Don't you remember me?"

Max's eyes widened.

Jake's heart nearly stopped.

The boy stepped closer.

"I was the one you left behind."

The boy stood in the middle of the elegant mirrored room, the light catching in his glassy eyes like he was part reflection, part reality. His voice echoed not just in the space—but in their minds.

Max stared at him, slowly stepping forward. "That's... not possible."

Jake's voice was barely a whisper. "You're dead."

The boy smiled—softly, sadly.

"No. Not quite. Not yet. Not entirely."

Sarah looked between them. "Okay, creepy cryptic ghost child, what the hell is going on?"

The boy tilted his head. "My name is Oliver. We were all here once, a long time ago. You were kids. Six years old. On a camping trip."

Sophie blinked. "What?"

Jake rubbed his temples. "This is crazy. We've never been here before."

Oliver took a step forward. The mirrors behind him shimmered, and suddenly, they weren't just reflecting the present anymore. They were projecting memories.

The mirror to the left showed four small children—Jake, Sophie, Max, and Sarah—running through the woods, giggling. The one on the right showed them stepping through the same twisted iron gate they'd just entered two nights ago.

Sarah gasped. "That's us."

Max backed up. "This is a trick. Another illusion."

"No," Oliver said, his voice cracking like glass. "It's the truth. You came here once before. We all did. Five of us. But only four of you left."

Sophie's knees buckled and she sat on the floor, trembling.

Jake slowly said, "We... forgot."

Oliver's face was pained. "The house made you forget. It erased your memories the moment you escaped. That was the cost. You left me behind. And I died."

Silence.

Heavy. Suffocating.

Max's voice shook. "We... we left you? We were just kids. We didn't know."

Oliver nodded. "But I've remembered every day since. Every night. And now I'm stuck here—half-alive, half-dead. The house fed on me. It used me. Turned me into the bait."

Sophie whispered, "That's why we were drawn back."

"You were the unfinished chapter," Oliver said. "You were the loose ends. You were the guilt they buried in your minds."

Jake stood up slowly. "Why now? Why are you telling us this?"

"Because I'm still in there," Oliver said, placing a hand on his chest. "Deep inside the mansion. Trapped. The version of me standing here is just a projection. An echo. A plea."

The mirrors rippled again—this time showing images of a dark basement filled with bones, cages, and a crooked throne made of children's toys.

"Is that where you are?" Sophie asked, eyes wide.

"Yes," Oliver said. "And if you don't come for me, if you leave again—the house will let you. But the price will be higher this time."

Sarah narrowed her eyes. "What price?"

Oliver's eyes flicked to Jake.

Jake swallowed hard.

"Death," Oliver said. "This time, one of you doesn't make it out. One of you has to stay behind. Just like I did."

Max threw his arms in the air. "Okay, plot twist much? We came here to not die, remember?"

Jake clenched his fists. "We can't let this happen again. We owe him. We owe ourselves. We can't keep running."

Sophie slowly stood beside him. "We finish what we started."

Sarah sighed and rolled her eyes. "Well, I always wanted to die somewhere that smelled like mildew and regret."

Max gave a weak laugh. "And I always thought the biggest twist in my life would be failing algebra."

They turned to Oliver.

"Where do we go?" Jake asked.

Oliver stepped back. The floor beneath them opened—not a hole, not a trap, but a spiral of light.

"A path," Oliver said. "But once you take it, the house will know your intent. It'll fight harder. Twist deeper. Feed on every last fear."

Sophie looked at the others. "Then we stay together. No matter what."

Max pointed at Sarah. "Even if she keeps being sarcastic."

Sarah smirked. "Especially if I keep being sarcastic."

Jake stepped toward the spiral. "Then let's go save a forgotten friend."

They jumped.

The spiral sucked them down—light twisting around them like a portal through time and trauma. Voices whispered in their ears.

"You left him."

"You forgot."

"You will forget again."

The spiral dumped them into a new room.

Or maybe not a room.

A playground.

But not just any playground—it was the playground. From their childhood.

Only now it was overgrown, broken, and scattered with ash. The swing set creaked though there was no wind. A merry-go-round spun slowly with no one on it. And a sandbox was filled with... bones.

Sophie walked toward the swing, entranced. "I know this place."

Jake whispered, "This is where we first met him."

Sarah bent down and picked up a toy shovel—rusted, cracked. Her initials were carved into the handle.

Max murmured, "The house is pulling us back through time. Making us remember. One memory at a time."

They turned.

At the end of the playground stood a shadowy figure.

Not Oliver.

But someone else.

It looked like a child at first—but the closer it got, the more wrong it became. Its limbs were too long. Its eyes were pitch black. Its mouth was sewn shut with golden thread.

Jake's breath caught in his throat. "That's not him. That's—"

The creature screamed.

And the entire world shattered like glass.

The scream ripped through the playground like a thunderclap, shattering the brittle silence and echoing into the depths of the mansion's cursed soul. The creature — no, the thing — lurched forward, long limbs flailing in unnatural jerks. Its sewn-shut mouth twitched as if it wanted to speak, but all that came out was a guttural hiss, like a broken toy trying desperately to scream.

Max shoved Sophie behind him, his heart hammering in his chest. "What the hell is that?"

Jake's gaze was fixed, his eyes narrowing as he recognized the familiar twisted form beneath the horror. "It's... it's what the house did to Oliver."

Sarah swallowed hard. "You mean... it's what it will do to us if we don't stop it?"

The thing advanced, dragging one twisted foot along the cracked pavement. Its eyes — endless pits of black — locked onto Jake, and a cold shiver slithered down his spine. The others instinctively closed ranks, but the creature seemed to ignore them, focused solely on Jake.

"You left me," it hissed, voice cracking like a brittle toy. "You left me here to rot."

Jake stepped forward, hands raised—not in defense, but pleading. "We didn't know. We were kids. We didn't remember."

The creature paused, the tension stretching until it snapped. Suddenly, it lunged — but instead of attacking, it reached out and grasped Jake's arm with a chilling grip. The touch burned like ice.

Jake gasped, feeling a coldness seep into his skin, crawling deeper with every second. His vision blurred; memories he'd long forgotten surged back — laughter around a campfire, the feel of warm hands holding his, Oliver's smile before the darkness swallowed him whole.

The others watched in horror as Jake's knees buckled. Sophie caught him just in time.

"You're marking him," Sarah whispered, voice trembling.

Max looked around frantically, trying to find a weapon, anything. "We have to stop this. Now."

But the creature's grip tightened, and Jake's body began to glow faintly with an eerie blue light. The house was claiming him — making its choice.

"No!" Sophie screamed, shaking him. "Jake, fight it!"

Jake's eyes fluttered open, filled with a mix of fear and determination. "You... you're not taking me. Not this time."

Summoning every ounce of strength, he wrenched his arm free. The creature stumbled back, snarling in frustration. But the damage was done — a mark glowed on Jake's wrist, like a brand burned into his skin.

Max gritted his teeth. "That's it. The house chose its sacrifice."

Sarah's voice was cold now. "We don't leave anyone behind. Not again."

Oliver's projection flickered nearby, fading in and out. "The path forward is through the basement. The heart of the house's darkness. That's where I am — and where the curse began."

Sophie wiped tears from her cheeks. "Then that's where we go."

With heavy hearts and trembling limbs, the four friends turned away from the haunted playground, descending a broken staircase that hadn't been there moments before. Each step echoed with memories and fears, pulling them deeper into the mansion's twisted grip.

As they reached the bottom, the air grew thick with decay and cold. The walls seemed to breathe, whispering secrets of pain and loss.

"Stay close," Jake ordered, flexing his marked wrist as if it gave him strength rather than fear.

The shadows flickered — and in the distance, a faint, sorrowful lullaby began to play.

The house wasn't done with them yet.

The basement stretched out before them like a cavernous tomb, walls slick with damp and streaked with strange symbols glowing faintly in the dark. The air smelled of earth and old sorrow, and every footstep echoed like a heartbeat — slow, steady, relentless.

Jake's wrist throbbed, the mark pulsing like a living thing beneath his skin. Sophie reached out and took his hand, grounding him. Max and Sarah flanked them both, weapons drawn — a broken chair leg, a rusted pipe, a flickering flashlight barely cutting through the gloom.

Oliver's voice, barely audible now, whispered in their minds. "The heart of the house is a prison — for memories, for souls, for the truth."

They moved deeper until they came to a heavy iron door, carved with scenes of children playing — and then screaming. The door creaked open under Max's push, revealing a room filled with light — but not the kind that brought comfort. This light was cold and clinical, emanating from strange machines and jars filled with cloudy liquid.

In the center, a throne made of children's toys — a grotesque monument — and beneath it, a faded portrait of a woman whose eyes seemed to bore into their souls.

Jake stepped forward. "Who was she?"

Oliver's voice answered. "The original mistress of the mansion. She was once a mother who lost her children — and in her grief, she cursed the land. The house was born from her sorrow and madness."

Sophie shivered. "So the mansion feeds on us because of her pain?"

"Yes. And it traps those who enter, to add to its power."

Suddenly, the machines whirred to life. The jars began to bubble, releasing whispers of trapped souls — the children who had come before, including Oliver.

"We have to break the curse," Sarah said, voice shaking but determined. "How?"

Oliver's image flickered, fading. "You must destroy the throne — the source of her power — but beware. The house will fight."

The room darkened as shadows twisted into monstrous forms. The house's final defense had awakened.

Jake raised the rusted pipe, stepping forward. "For Oliver. For us."

The battle for their lives—and their souls—had begun.

VI

The Curse Beneath the Floorboards

The moment Jake brought the rusted pipe down on the throne of toys, everything exploded.

Not literally. But the air cracked like thunder. Light shattered. And the floor beneath them screamed.

Yes. Screamed.

The throne erupted in a gust of cold, shadowy wind, sending shattered plastic soldiers, headless dolls, and melted Lego bricks flying in all directions. The house didn't just moan in protest—it roared, furious, betrayed, like a living creature wounded in its core.

"YEP!" Max shouted, ducking as a Barbie head whizzed past him. "THE TOY QUEEN IS MAD!"

"RUN!" Jake bellowed.

The four teens bolted as the walls of the basement began to buckle, bones rattling from the shelves, jars exploding like they were popcorn kernels in hell's microwave. The staircase they'd come down moments ago was gone—swallowed by darkness like it had never existed.

Behind them, the shadows from the walls peeled off and chased like a tidal wave made of smoke and screams.

They sprinted through the crumbling hallways, turning corners blindly. Sophie led, Jake just behind her despite the painful glow of the mark on his arm. Sarah clutched Max's hand, half-running, half-dragging him.

"What now?!" Sarah gasped, swatting away a flying marionette puppet.

Jake shouted, "Find another way up! We need to get back to the—"

The floor gave way.

Again.

For the third time since entering this nightmare, they plummeted—this time into a room that defied all logic.

They landed on thick, velvet carpet in a space that looked like an old Victorian nursery, only it was massive—mansion-sized. Toy trains rode loops along the walls, rocking horses creaked by themselves, and dolls blinked.

All at once.

In sync.

Sophie sat up, her hair tangled and her shirt streaked with soot. "You've gotta be kidding me."

Jake looked around. "No way this was part of the original floor plan."

Sarah kicked a doll off her foot. "I swear this place has more trap doors than plot holes in teen slasher films."

Max blinked at a stuffed bear, which blinked back. "I'm not dying in a baby room. Not happening."

Suddenly, the trains stopped. The horses froze mid-rock. And the dolls all turned their heads.

Toward Jake.

He groaned. "Let me guess. They want me."

The mark on his wrist was glowing again, brighter this time, casting eerie blue light over the room.

One doll twitched and opened its mouth. "You're marked. You're chosen."

Sophie got in front of Jake, fists up like she was about to punch porcelain. "He's not yours. Try me, freakshow."

Max grabbed a wooden crib and yanked off a spindle. "Sophie, I love the violent energy. Big fan."

Jake's voice was calm but cold. "If I'm the one this house wants—then fine. But we're ending this on our terms."

"Absolutely not," Sophie snapped. "Don't even think about being a noble idiot."

Sarah rolled her eyes. "Can we not have a tragic sacrifice speech right now?"

"I'm not sacrificing myself," Jake said, locking eyes with Sophie. "Not yet. Not until we destroy whatever's keeping this curse alive. And not until we bring Oliver home."

Suddenly, a faint humming noise filled the room—a lullaby. The same one from earlier. The one from their childhood.

Jake's breath caught.

"That song..." Sophie whispered. "I... I remember it."

They all froze.

Bits and pieces of a memory began to form in their minds. A night long ago. A campfire. A game of hide and seek. A daring challenge. A foggy path that led to the mansion. The laughter. The fear. Oliver's voice calling out.

And then... nothing. Blackness. The house had wiped it all clean.

Until now.

The dolls began to fall over. The room started to flicker, like the house was losing control.

Max looked around. "What's happening?"

Sophie whispered, "We're remembering. And the house can't handle that."

With a groan of ancient wood, a hidden door creaked open behind the rocking horse. Beyond it? A hallway they hadn't seen before, lined with oil portraits and candlelight. At the end: a spiral staircase heading upward.

Jake stood. "That's our way out."

"Are you sure?" Sarah asked.

Jake nodded. "I don't know why… but I am."

They moved quickly, climbing the staircase, the humming fading behind them. The higher they went, the warmer the air became, the more familiar the architecture. They were heading back to the mansion's upper floors—maybe even the entrance.

At the top, they emerged into a massive ballroom.

Everything was silent.

Empty.

But not abandoned.

In the center stood a woman.

Tall. Pale. Wearing a black mourning gown from another century. Her eyes were hollow, but her presence was suffocating. And around her, hovering like wisps of smoke, were the souls of dozens of children—flickering, glowing, and whispering.

The grieving mother.

Sophie stepped forward. "Are you the one who cursed this place?"

The woman didn't blink. "I lost everything. So I made this house to keep what little I had left."

Jake stepped beside her. "You kept them prisoner."

"I kept them safe," she snapped. "From the world. From forgetting."

Max muttered, "Oh great. A ghost with abandonment issues."

The woman's dress fluttered without wind. "You came back to finish what you started. But the price remains."

Her gaze fell to Jake.

"The mark has chosen."

Sophie's voice cracked. "Then unchoose him."

Sarah added, "Yeah, lady, he's taken."

Jake stood his ground. "You made this place to preserve memory. But you've made it a tomb. That's not love. That's control."

The woman's face contorted with rage. The children around her wailed.

The room darkened.

"Then join them," she hissed.

The final showdown had begun.

The ballroom exploded into chaos.

The chandelier overhead shattered, raining down shards of glass like frozen daggers. The floor cracked beneath their feet, tendrils of shadow snaking up from the marble like the mansion itself had opened its eyes.

And in the center of it all—her black gown billowing like storm clouds—the woman floated above them, arms outstretched, face twisted in grief and fury.

"I offered you memory," she wailed, voice booming through the vast hall. "And you dare refuse?"

Jake shielded Sophie as a gust of shadow slammed into them. He gritted his teeth, but stayed standing. "No offense, but your version of 'memory lane' comes with too many corpses."

Max grabbed a candelabra off the wall and swung it like a baseball bat. "I say we evict this lady now!"

With an inhuman shriek, the ghostly woman sent the children's souls flying toward the teens—spinning through the air like glowing comets, eyes wide, arms outstretched.

"They're not attacking," Sophie gasped. "They're—trapped."

Jake nodded. "She's using them as shields."

Sarah narrowed her eyes. "If we set them free, we weaken her."

"Okay," Max said, readying the candelabra like a knight with a very fancy torch. "How do we do that? Just slap them and say 'be free?'"

Sophie looked around wildly, then spotted the ancient piano near the edge of the ballroom. "The lullaby."

Jake blinked. "What?"

"The song we remembered. It's the key. It's what she sang to them before trapping them. Maybe if we reverse it..."

Max groaned. "Of course. Because nothing says horror like musical exorcism."

Sophie sprinted to the piano, brushing off dust and cracking her knuckles like she was about to enter a demonic talent show. "Let's hope I remember Mrs. Geller's lessons from fifth grade."

The piano groaned as she struck the keys—off-key at first, but then the haunting lullaby started to unravel backward. The air shifted instantly. The ghost children paused mid-flight, their eyes clearing, glowing less blue and more human.

The spirit let out a piercing scream, whipping toward Sophie. "NO!"

Jake lunged between them. "Touch her and I swear, ghost or not, I will make you re-dead."

With each note Sophie played, more of the children slowed, blinking, gasping—as if waking up from centuries of nightmare.

Max charged at the spirit, swinging the candelabra with heroic idiocy. "Come at me, Victorian Voldemort!"

Sarah followed, lighting one of the candle tips with her lighter. "Let's see how you handle fire, you floating funeral!"

The spirit hissed, retreating slightly—her form flickering.

Sophie kept playing, her fingers trembling but focused. "Almost there—just a few more bars—"

The chandelier remnants began to swirl around the room like a tornado of glass. Jake raised the rusted pipe and screamed back at the howling wind. "We're ending this! This house doesn't own us anymore!"

Suddenly, the ghost children all stopped midair. Every single one of them looked at the ghost woman and said—in unison—"Let us go."

And then—

They vanished.

All of them. Gone.

The ghost woman collapsed to her knees, her entire form dimming. Her rage crumbled, replaced by an unbearable sadness.

"They were all I had…" she whispered.

Jake stepped forward. "You lost your kids. I get that. But you stole everyone else's. That's not grief. That's punishment."

She looked up at him, her face softening for the first time. "You're the boy who remembered."

"I wish I hadn't."

Her ghostly hand reached out—not threatening now, just tired. She pressed it to his chest, over his heart. "Then remember for me."

A final pulse of blue light flashed—and then she was gone.

No scream. No final curse. Just silence.

The room brightened. The cracked floor sealed. The portraits on the walls smiled for the first time.

Max dropped the candelabra with a loud clang. "Is it over?"

Sophie blinked. "It feels like it."

Sarah turned to Jake. "The mark...?"

Jake looked down.

Gone.

No glow. No burn. Just skin.

He laughed—quiet, almost shocked. "I think we did it."

They all stood there for a moment, dazed, dirty, bruised—but alive.

Sophie collapsed into Jake's arms. "That was so dumb. You almost got ghost-napped."

Jake hugged her tightly. "You saved me. With a piano. That's weirdly hot."

Max sat down, legs shaking. "I am never playing Monopoly in an old building ever again."

Sarah flopped next to him. "Or Ouija. Or Jenga. Or even Scrabble."

They found a door that led, somehow, back to the entry hall. It was... normal now. The walls weren't bleeding. The chandeliers weren't growling. It felt like a house again.

Outside, dawn had started to break.

They stepped out into the jungle, morning birds chirping like they hadn't just survived literal supernatural war.

As they walked toward the trail back to town, Jake turned around one last time.

The mansion stood there, silent. Watching.

And then—

It blinked out of sight.

Gone.

Vanished.

Like it had never existed.

Max let out a hysterical laugh. "Okay! Cool! I'm mentally unwell now!"

Sophie laughed. "At least you're consistent."

Sarah put a hand on Jake's shoulder. "So... what now?"

Jake looked at them all—his friends, his family, his fellow idiots.

"We go home."

VII

Home, Sweet Haunted Home

Jake's jaw tightened. "That's not the mansion."

"No kidding," Max muttered. "Ours had… less sunlight, more screaming wallpaper."

They trudged down the main road, sticking to the edge like fugitives who just escaped a nightmare—which, technically, they had. The school bus stop came into view, still perfectly intact, graffiti and all. A middle-aged guy jogged past them in neon shorts, earbuds in, giving a friendly wave. "Morning, kids!"

Jake stared after him. "Seriously?"

Sophie's voice dropped to a whisper. "He didn't notice… we look like we fought a tornado inside a blender."

Sarah stepped toward the street, eyeing the town like it was wearing a disguise. "It's like they don't remember. Like the town's been scrubbed clean."

Max nodded slowly. "Like we're the only ones who know the real version."

Jake frowned. "Or the only ones who came back from it."

They kept walking. At first glance, Glenridge looked fine. Too fine. Main Street was bustling. The bakery's "Fresh Muffins Today!"

sign waved in the breeze. The hardware store had a banner for a Father's Day hammer sale. Nothing was out of place... except for them.

Then came the second warning.

As they passed the town's museum—normally closed before 10 a.m.—the door creaked open by itself.

Jake stopped dead. "Okay. That's not normal."

Sophie stared into the shadows inside the museum. "We're not going in there, right?"

A loud thud echoed from within.

Max raised an eyebrow. "That was either a friendly ghost... or a homicidal librarian."

Another thud. Then, a whisper—barely audible but unmistakable.

"Sophie..."

Everyone froze.

Jake grabbed Sophie's hand without thinking. "Okay. We're leaving. Immediately."

The door slammed shut behind them as they backed away. The street was still. No one else had heard it. No one reacted.

Not even the jogger, now stretching by the lamppost like nothing had happened.

Max slowly turned in a circle. "So we didn't leave the nightmare. We just changed the location."

Sarah rubbed her arms, chilled despite the morning sun. "What if the mansion didn't vanish? What if it followed us?"

Jake shook his head. "No, that place was bound. We watched it disappear."

Sophie glanced behind them, heart thudding. "What if it didn't disappear... what if it just moved in?"

They finally reached Sophie's house. Her front yard was still littered with pink garden gnomes and a birdbath shaped like a cat. Everything looked untouched. Familiar.

But the porch light was on.

At 8 a.m.

Sophie's face paled. "That light only comes on at night. When someone's waiting for me."

Jake walked up beside her. "You want me to knock?"

She nodded.

He raised his hand to knock, but the door creaked open first.

Inside stood Sophie's mom.

She smiled brightly. "Hi, Jake! Sophie! Come in—you're just in time for breakfast!"

Max blinked. "Okay. Are we being gaslit by pancakes?"

Sarah squinted. "Her mom looks exactly the same. Not worried. Not suspicious. Not even surprised."

Jake stepped cautiously inside. The kitchen smelled like bacon and cinnamon. A stack of pancakes sizzled on the griddle. Her mom hummed as she flipped one expertly.

Sophie hesitated. "Mom... how long have I been gone?"

Her mom smiled without turning around. "What do you mean, sweetie? You were just upstairs. I told you to wake your friends for breakfast."

Jake's voice was quiet. "We haven't been upstairs. We've been in a haunted mansion for days."

Her mom finally turned, spatula in hand. "Jake, don't be silly. You kids and your stories."

Max stepped in. "Wait. Does she think we had a sleepover? Like... last night?"

Sarah poked at her own cheek. "I still have claw marks from a cursed Victorian bedframe. Does that look like a sleepover injury?"

Jake grabbed Sophie's hand again. Her pulse was racing.

Sophie's mom's smile didn't change. But her eyes did.

Just for a second.

Too wide. Too blank.

And then: "Syrup?"

Max screamed and ducked behind a chair.

They bolted.

Outside, Jake took a deep breath, trying to make sense of it. "She's not her mom. She's... something else."

"Or controlled," Sophie whispered. "Like the town's under some kind of curse."

Sarah looked up at the sky. "And we're the only ones immune?"

Jake turned toward the town square. "We need help."

They made their way to Glenridge High, thinking maybe the teachers—someone—would notice something was wrong.

Instead, the school was already full of students. Normal. Casual. Laughing. Shoving books in lockers. Playing basketball.

Sophie scanned the hallway. "Is this some kind of supernatural Truman Show?"

Jake stopped dead as a familiar figure passed by.

"Wait... that's Coach Davis."

"Yeah?" Max said.

Jake grabbed his arm. "Coach Davis died. Remember? Back in Chapter 3. Slaughtered by the painting."

They all turned to look.

Coach Davis walked right past them. Whistling. Carrying a clipboard.

Sarah's eyes went wide. "That's not possible."

Jake stepped forward. "Coach!"

The man turned, smiling. "Hey there, champ. Ready for the big game?"

Jake blinked. "What... game?"

"The homecoming game. Friday night, remember?"

The man clapped him on the back and walked off.

Jake turned slowly to the others. "Okay. Something really messed up is happening."

Max looked pale. "We're in a town that doesn't know we ever left. People who died are alive. And we're the only ones who know."

Sarah pulled out her phone. "I'm calling my dad."

Static.

Max tried his. "No bars. No Wi-Fi. No hope."

Jake's phone buzzed.

One new message.

"Welcome home. Don't forget us."

No number. No sender.

Attached was a photo—grainy, faded, but real.

The four of them.

Standing in front of the mansion.

As children.

Jake stared at it.

They were maybe six or seven years old. All holding hands. All smiling.

Max gasped. "Wait... is that—us?"

Sarah grabbed the phone. "This can't be real."

Sophie looked like her soul had left her body. "I... I remember this. A field trip. To the old house. Years ago."

Jake clutched his head. "We've been there before. The mansion erased our memories. Until now."

Max swore. "So this is some kind of sick return trip?"

Sarah nodded. "We were brought back."

Jake whispered, "Maybe... to finish what we started."

That night, they didn't go home. They couldn't. They met in the town cemetery, the one place that still felt untouched.

Max showed up last, dragging a backpack full of snacks and candles. "If we're gonna fight ghost-town 2.0, I'm doing it with beef jerky and firelight."

Sophie sat next to Jake on a gravestone. "This isn't over, is it?"

Jake shook his head. "We left the mansion. But the mansion didn't leave us."

Sarah lit a candle. "We need answers. And fast."

The candle flickered violently in the wind.

And from the trees beyond the cemetery...

A whisper:

"You came back. Just like before."

VIII
The Candy Lady's Return

The night wrapped the mansion in a shroud thicker than any blanket, an oppressive darkness that seemed to press down on their chests, making every breath a deliberate effort. Jake, Sophie, Max, and Sarah stood just beyond the crumbling iron gate, the twisted vines clutching its bars like greedy fingers. The mansion loomed before them, a gaping maw of shadows and peeling paint, its silhouette jagged and cruel against the storm-dark sky.

Sophie pulled her jacket tighter around her, trying to ignore the tremble in her hands. "So we really have to go back inside? After everything that happened, you want to risk it all again?"

Jake's voice was steady, though inside he felt a war of nerves. "We have no choice. Whatever this place is, it's still messing with our heads. If we don't face it, it won't ever let us go."

Max scoffed, kicking a loose stone. "Face it? The last time we faced it, I thought we were dead three times over. And here I am, still covered in scratches and bruises."

Sarah rolled her eyes, but the edge of fear in her voice betrayed her bravado. "Look, the house already knows us. It remembers. Maybe if we go back, we can figure out what it wants... or better yet, find a way out of this nightmare."

The mansion's door creaked open with a tortured groan as if inviting them inside to play some twisted game. Their footsteps crunched over dead leaves and shattered glass on the porch. Inside, the air was thick with dust and a faint, sickly sweet scent that made Sophie's stomach churn. The walls were lined with faded wallpaper peeling in long strips, and the floorboards moaned underfoot, every creak echoing like a whispered warning.

A faint flicker of candlelight danced at the end of a long hallway, casting strange shadows that slithered and shifted. Sophie's heart thudded painfully in her chest. "Did you guys see that?"

Jake nodded grimly. "Yeah. Something's here."

As they moved forward, the mansion seemed to breathe around them, the walls closing in, the shadows lengthening. Suddenly, a chorus of childish giggles echoed from the darkness—a sound so innocent yet dripping with malice that it made the hairs on their necks stand on end.

Max swallowed hard. "That's... not possible. Nobody should be here."

But the giggles morphed into whispering voices, calling their names, tugging at their memories like threads unraveling. Sophie felt herself slipping, the edges of her reality blurring as visions of their lost childhood visits flickered behind her eyes—the laughter, the fear, the promises they never meant to keep.

Then she saw her: the Candy Lady. Pale as moonlight, with eyes as black as night, lips curved into a smile too wide, too sharp. She held out a hand, inviting, coaxing. "Welcome back, children. It's time to play."

The mansion erupted into chaos—the floor cracked open, walls bleeding shadows, the air thick with screams and laughter intertwined. They ran, stumbling through hallways that twisted and morphed, the house trying to trap them in its nightmare web.

Jake grabbed Sophie's hand, their fingers interlacing tightly as they fought to remember who they were beneath the fear. "We end this. Together."

As they burst through the front doors into the storm's cold rain, the Candy Lady's laughter chased them into the night. But beneath the terror, something else stirred—a spark of hope that maybe, just maybe, they could break free from the mansion's grasp once and for all.

The rain was a cold slap against their skin, soaking through their clothes and chilling them to the bone, but none of them cared. All that mattered was escaping the suffocating nightmare inside the mansion's walls. Sophie's heart hammered as she glanced back, half-expecting to see the Candy Lady's pale face grinning at the doorway, but the house had fallen silent once more, as if it was gathering strength for the next move.

Max wiped water from his eyes, panting heavily. "This is insane. We're just running in circles, but the house never really lets us go."

Jake's jaw was clenched tight. "It's not just the house. It's whatever curse or magic is tied to it—and to us."

Sarah shivered, her teeth chattering despite the adrenaline. "You think it's tied to our memories? Like the whole thing started the day we forgot we'd even been here?"

Sophie swallowed the lump in her throat. "I keep thinking about those flashes... moments of us as kids, scared and confused but somehow connected. Maybe the mansion is feeding on that forgotten pain."

Jake stared up at the black sky. "Or maybe it's trying to make us remember, but on its own terms."

The wind picked up, howling through the skeletal trees, carrying whispers that seemed almost human—pleading, threatening, promising things no sane person would want. The mansion behind them groaned, like a beast disturbed from a long sleep.

Sophie suddenly stopped, clutching Jake's arm. "Wait... do you hear that?"

A soft, melodic humming floated through the air, a lullaby twisted into something dark and hypnotic. It wasn't coming from the house—it was coming from inside their heads. Memories clawed at their minds, jumbled and painful.

Jake squeezed her hand. "Stay with me."

They followed the sound, which led them deeper into the overgrown garden surrounding the mansion, where moonflowers bloomed eerily under the moonlight, their petals glowing faintly like ghostly lanterns. In the center of the garden stood a cracked fountain, water long dried up, but the hum seemed to originate there.

Max bent down and touched the cracked stone. "This place... it's the heart of the mansion, isn't it?"

Suddenly, the ground trembled and a whisper echoed from the shadows, "Remember..."

Sophie's vision blurred as the memories flooded in—a long-ago summer, laughter ringing through these very gardens, the four of them as children sharing secrets and candy, promising to be friends forever. But then the skies darkened, the laughter turned to screams, and the mansion loomed as a trap, swallowing their innocence whole.

She gasped, tears mixing with the rain. "We weren't just lost. We were trapped. And we forgot because it hurt too much."

Jake looked at them all, pain and resolve battling in his eyes. "Then it's time to face the truth, no matter how dark."

As they stood there, the garden shifted. The shadows coalesced into twisted shapes—faces from their past, twisted memories of childhood fears and forgotten promises. The Candy Lady stepped forward again, her voice cold and deadly sweet. "You cannot run from what you are."

Sarah swallowed, her voice barely a whisper. "Then what do we do?"

Jake squared his shoulders. "We fight. For our memories, for our friendship, for our lives."

The mansion's walls trembled as if preparing for the final battle. But this time, the four were ready to face the nightmare together.

Thunder cracked overhead like a warning shot from the heavens as the mansion's front garden transformed into something unholy. The vines coiled like snakes, the trees shifted positions like chess pieces on a board, and the Candy Lady now floated above the cracked fountain, her black dress rippling despite the still air.

Her voice echoed in layers, childlike and ancient all at once. "You broke the rules. You left before the game was finished."

Max took a shaky step forward, his hands clenched. "That's because we didn't know we were playing your freakshow of a game!"

The Candy Lady smiled, her teeth too many and too sharp. "Ignorance is not an excuse. You were mine from the start. And now that you remember... you're mine again."

Sophie's eyes blazed with sudden fire. "We were kids. You tricked us. You scared us into forgetting. But not this time."

The four of them stood shoulder to shoulder as the ground beneath the fountain split open with a violent roar, revealing a spiral staircase leading down into darkness. From that pit surged dozens of shadowy children—translucent, sobbing, whispering—half-real, half-memory. The Candy Lady spread her arms wide, as if orchestrating an opera of torment.

Jake narrowed his eyes. "She feeds on fear. Our fear. That's how she keeps us tied here."

Sarah shook her head. "Then let's starve her."

Before anyone could respond, Jake took a step toward the Candy Lady and said the one thing none of them expected.

"I forgive you."

The Candy Lady paused. Her head twitched, her smile faltering.

Jake continued, louder this time. "I forgive you. For tricking us. For feeding on our fear. For every twisted game you played."

Sophie saw it first—the flicker of confusion in the woman's endless black eyes. The shadows paused mid-surge, uncertain.

Max caught on. "Yeah. Same here. You messed with our heads, sure, but we forgive you."

Sarah gave a little smirk, arms crossed. "Not because you deserve it. Because we do."

The Candy Lady screamed—a sound that tore through the fabric of the night, ripping clouds apart and sending the spectral children scattering. Her form shimmered, flickered, then began to unravel, like ash in the wind.

"No... no! You can't! You were MINE!"

But it was too late.

The mansion groaned as if in agony, its walls buckling, windows shattering inward. Light erupted from the garden fountain and the spiral staircase imploded into itself. The Candy Lady's shriek echoed one final time before she exploded into a mist of black petals, vanishing into the storm.

Then—

Silence.

Rain still fell. The wind still whispered through the trees. But the weight was gone. The mansion behind them was no longer pulsing with dread. Its windows were dark, its heartbeat finally still.

Max sank to his knees, soaked and shaking. "Did we just... win?"

Jake didn't answer. He simply fell to the grass, lying on his back and staring at the clouds parting above. Sophie joined him, her head on his chest, her fingers still laced in his.

Sarah stood near the broken fountain, staring into its now-glowing waters. Reflected inside weren't their current selves—but their childhood versions, happy and together, untouched by fear.

She smiled. "We remembered. That's what beat her."

Jake murmured, "And that we're still idiots... but we're idiots together."

They laughed, exhausted and soaked, but somehow lighter than they had felt since entering that cursed place.

But unknown to them, deep inside the mansion, far below the rotting floorboards, something else stirred. A mirror cracked. A forgotten name whispered. And a pale doll's eye blinked once.

The house wasn't done. Not yet.

IX

The Mirror That Saw
Too Much

It began with a whisper.

Not one of those dramatic ghost whispers with howling wind and echo effects—no, this was subtler. The kind of whisper that slithered just beneath the skin, teasing the edge of your hearing, making you question if you'd even heard it at all. Sophie jerked her head toward the hallway.

"Did someone just say my name?" she whispered, eyes narrowing like a cat spotting a laser dot.

Jake paused mid-bite on a suspiciously crunchy granola bar (which they had scavenged from a dusty pantry labeled "DO NOT EAT IF YOU VALUE YOUR LIFE"). He chewed once more, slowly. "Unless Max has learned ventriloquism in the last fifteen minutes, I don't think so."

"I can try," Max said helpfully, then threw his voice. "Sophie... I am the ghost of lactose intolerant cheese... Beware my dairy wrath..."

Sophie threw the empty granola wrapper at him.

Sarah, meanwhile, wasn't laughing. She was staring ahead, toward a large door that none of them remembered being there before. It looked... newer than the rest. Not clean-new. More like freshly-unsealed-coffin-new.

"Guys," she said. "That wasn't there before, right?"

Everyone turned. Jake blinked. "Nope."

"Definitely nope," Max added, stepping protectively in front of the girls. "And that... uh... totally doesn't look like a cursed vampire mirror room or anything."

"Max," Sarah said flatly, "how would you even know what a cursed vampire mirror room looks like?"

"I play Dungeons & Dragons. I'm practically a scholar in cursed furniture."

Jake stepped forward and placed his hand against the door. Cold. Definitely not normal cold either—this was refrigerator-after-a-power-outage cold. He turned to the others, "We going in?"

Max shrugged. "If we say no, the door will open on its own later and trap us anyway, right?"

"Classic horror move," Sophie agreed. "Let's just get this over with."

And so, naturally, they entered.

The room was circular, domed at the top, with cracked marble floors and a dozen tall mirrors arranged like an audience. No lights, no windows. Yet somehow, the entire space glowed with an eerie bluish hue. The mirrors shimmered faintly. Not from any reflection—because none of them showed the group's reflections.

Instead, they showed... memories.

Jake stared at the first mirror. It showed a little boy crying on a swing set, covered in mud, alone at recess. A girl with scraped knees—blonde, loud, and adorable—ran up and offered a bandage. Jake flinched.

"That's... me," he whispered.

Sophie was looking at a different mirror. It played like a movie reel: her, sitting on the floor of a sunlit classroom, shyly offering a broken cookie to a boy with wild brown hair.

"That's Max," she said, voice barely audible.

Max and Sarah turned to their own mirrors. Sarah's showed a younger version of herself clumsily chasing a squirrel at a park while two boys—Jake and Max—egged her on, and a little girl, clearly Sophie, tried to catch up. Max's mirror flickered rapidly between scenes: the four of them climbing trees, building a makeshift fort, then later, much later—running through this very mansion as children.

And that's when the memories stopped being sweet.

One mirror cracked as it showed the children screaming.

Another trembled as it displayed shadowy figures dragging one of the kids—Max, by the looks of it—down a hallway.

A third glitched out, overloading with static.

Then, slowly, each mirror began to show the same scene in sync: the kids—Jake, Sophie, Max, and Sarah—running, terrified, through a burning library. The walls melted like wax. The shadows swallowed them.

Then everything went dark.

The mirrors froze on one final image: the four children, unconscious in front of the mansion gates. An old woman with pale skin and soulless eyes stood behind them, her long, claw-like fingers dripping with something that looked a lot like blood.

"WHAT... THE HELL... WAS THAT?" Max yelled, stepping back and bumping into Sarah, who was white as a sheet.

"We were here before," Sarah whispered, clutching her arms. "As kids... this place... it wiped our memories."

"No," Jake said slowly, piecing it together. "It didn't wipe them. It buried them. Deep. This room just—dug them up."

Sophie was frozen. Her hand trembled as she pointed to one mirror—the only one that hadn't gone dark. It was still playing, but not a memory.

It was now.

In the mirror, they saw themselves. Not as they were now—but as they would be.

Max was screaming. Sarah was being dragged into the shadows. Jake was bleeding—badly. Sophie was standing alone, eyes hollow, holding something in her hands.

Something... red.

"I don't want to see this anymore," Sophie whispered. "Make it stop."

But the mirrors weren't listening.

Suddenly, the doors slammed shut behind them, and every mirror exploded.

Shards rained down. Jake dove and shielded Sophie with his body, while Max pulled Sarah behind a collapsed pedestal. When the sound finally died down, the silence was deafening.

Then the laughter started.

It came from the shards.

Hundreds of tiny voices cackled from every broken piece. Whispering names. Their names.

"Sophie..."

"Jake..."

"Max..."

"Sarah..."

"RUN."

They didn't need to be told twice.

The four bolted through the smoke and debris. Jake was limping slightly, a shallow cut on his thigh bleeding. Sophie was holding onto his arm tightly, her hands shaking. Sarah looked like she'd been dunked in ice water. Max... was unusually quiet.

They ran until they found a narrow passage, one that hadn't been there before. It led downward—spiraling like a corkscrew into the depths of the mansion.

"Nope, nope, NOPE—stairs that go underground are never a good sign," Max said. "This is like the express lane to demonville."

Jake wiped the sweat from his brow. "We stay here, we die. We go down... maybe we just mostly die."

"I choose mostly," Sophie muttered, pulling him along.

The descent felt endless. The air got thicker. Colder. Max kept humming horror movie soundtracks nervously, until Sarah snapped, "If you hum The Exorcist theme one more time, I swear I'll throw you down myself."

Finally, they reached the bottom. It opened into a massive, dark chamber.

In the center: a mirror.

Tall, arched like a cathedral window, framed in twisted black metal that pulsed like veins. This one wasn't cracked. And unlike the others, it did reflect them.

Jake stepped forward.

"Why do I feel like this is the boss level?"

Then the mirror spoke.

Not in words. Not aloud. But directly into their minds.

"One must give what was taken. One must see what was hidden. One must die for the rest to live."

Sophie gritted her teeth. "Why is it always riddles with evil entities? Why can't it ever be something normal, like 'do five jumping jacks and we'll let you go'?"

The mirror shimmered, showing flickering versions of themselves—older, broken, twisted. Sophie with empty eyes. Max chained to a wall. Sarah floating above the ground, her hair moving as if underwater. Jake—missing.

"No," Jake said firmly. "We're not playing this game."

But Sarah stepped closer, her voice soft. "What if we already played it? When we were kids. What if one of us already died back then... and the mirror just brought us back wrong?"

Max stared at the image of himself chained and broken. "If that's the case, I want a damn refund."

Sophie turned to Jake. "Do you think we're still alive? Like... really alive? Or is this some weird... memory loop?"

Jake looked at her, then slowly reached out to touch the mirror.

His fingers went through.

Just like water.

"Portal," he muttered. "Or... trap."

"Or both," Max added. "Like a portal-trap combo meal. Comes with fries and trauma."

They stood there, uncertain. The mirror pulsed again.

"Choose."

The room began to shake. Dust fell from the ceiling.

Jake turned to them. "We either go through this thing or we let the house collapse on us. I vote we move forward."

Max hesitated. Then nodded. "If we die, I'm haunting you all."

"One problem," Sarah said. "What if the 'one must die' part is literal?"

The mirror flickered—then showed Jake, stepping alone through the portal. The others remained behind.

Jake backed away, swallowing. "Well, that's comforting."

Sophie grabbed his hand. "If anyone's dying, it's not you. Not yet."

Jake smiled at her, and for a moment, the terror lifted.

Then Sophie stepped forward.

And jumped.

Straight into the mirror.

"SOPHIE!" Jake screamed.

The mirror flared bright red.

Max lunged forward, but Sarah held him back. "WAIT. Look!"

The mirror cleared.

On the other side, Sophie was standing unharmed... inside what looked like the mansion—but different. Cleaner. Brighter. Familiar.

She turned and beckoned to them.

"Come on," she said, her voice echoing from the other side. "I think I found the way out."

Jake didn't wait. He ran after her, diving into the mirror.

Then Max.

Then Sarah.

The chamber collapsed behind them.

And the mirror—the cursed mirror—shattered for the last time.

Sophie gritted her teeth. "Why is it always something about dying? Why can't it ever be like, 'solve this mildly confusing crossword puzzle and you'll be free'?"

The mirror shimmered.

A cold gust swept the chamber, lifting Max's hoodie slightly and making Sarah gasp. Shadows spilled from the edges of the mirror like leaking ink, slithering across the floor. They moved unnaturally, curling around their feet but not quite touching—like predators circling prey, savoring the fear.

Jake squinted. "The mirror said—'one must give what was taken'? What does that mean?"

"Maybe it wants back the memories," Sarah guessed, backing away as the shadows brushed her boots. "Like... the ones it showed us upstairs. Maybe we were never supposed to see them again."

"I don't think it's asking for permission," Max muttered. "It's hungry. It wants more than memories."

A tendril of shadow reached for Sophie.

Jake shoved her behind him instinctively.

The mirror pulsed.

Suddenly, Jake's reflection stepped out of the mirror. Except—it wasn't quite Jake.

His doppelgänger was twisted slightly. Not grotesquely—but just enough to be wrong. His smile was a little too wide. His eyes, a little too dark. His voice, too smooth as it said:

"You remember now, don't you, Jake? How you brought them here. How you promised them it would be fun."

Jake froze. "No... I didn't."

Sophie looked at him, confused. "Jake...?"

But the mirror version kept speaking, circling them. "You dared them to come through the gate. You led them inside. You knew the stories. You wanted to prove them wrong."

"That's not true," Jake whispered. "That's not how I remember it..."

"Because I am your memory," the reflection hissed. "I'm what you buried."

Jake clenched his fists. "I was eight. I didn't know."

Sophie stepped beside him, glaring at the doppelgänger. "Whatever happened back then—it wasn't his fault."

Mirror-Jake tilted his head. "But someone has to pay."

With a scream, the shadow-Jake lunged at them.

Sarah and Max scattered. Jake tackled his double to the ground, wrestling with something that felt like sludge and steel at once. It snarled in his face, its features shifting rapidly between versions of himself—angry, scared, laughing maniacally.

"Get off him!" Sophie screamed, picking up a loose chunk of rock and smashing it into the thing's back.

The shadow hissed and slithered away like water, reforming in front of the mirror.

Then Sarah screamed.

Max turned to see another reflection stepping out—himself.

Max's shadow twin walked with a slight limp and carried a broken Rubik's Cube, identical to the one Max used to fidget with in middle school.

It smiled, then said, "Still hiding behind the jokes, huh? Still pretending you don't care?"

Max took a step back. "I... I don't..."

"Liar."

The room darkened again.

One by one, their mirror selves began to emerge.

Sophie's was silent but sobbing—clutching a music box and muttering her name over and over.

Sarah's walked with grace but had hollow eyes—staring straight at the real Sarah with utter disappointment.

They were surrounded.

Max backed into Sophie. "Okay, okay, maybe the crossword puzzle death trap isn't sounding so bad anymore."

Jake panted, glancing around. "This is what it meant. One must give. One must see. One must die..."

"Why are we always candidates for that last part?" Max hissed.

"We can't fight them," Sarah said, voice trembling but steady. "They're us. Our guilt. Our past. We have to face it."

"How?" Sophie asked, tears welling. "We don't even remember what we did wrong!"

But something inside Jake clicked.

"No… we do," he said. "We just don't want to."

He turned to the central mirror and shouted, "Show us the truth."

The chamber trembled.

The mirror pulsed violently, shadows recoiling.

Then—one final vision appeared.

It showed the children—young Jake, Sophie, Max, and Sarah—sneaking into the mansion, giggling, daring each other to go deeper. They entered a sealed room. The same mirror stood there, waiting.

They stared at it. Touched it.

And one by one, they disappeared inside it.

Except Jake.

He was the last one out. Barely.

He had yanked Sophie out just in time, her screams echoing. Sarah and Max had emerged differently—unconscious, injured, cold. And then—Jake made a deal.

The woman appeared again. The pale one. Her voice was like nails tapping on glass.

"Leave… and forget. But when you remember… one must return."

Jake had agreed. A selfish, desperate little boy trying to save his friends.

Back in the present, Jake collapsed to his knees.

"I did bring us here," he said. "I knew. Somewhere in me—I always knew."

Sophie dropped beside him. "You were a child. You didn't choose this."

"I made the deal," Jake whispered. "And now it's time to pay."

"No," Max said, stepping between them. "We find another way. There's always another way."

The mirror began to crack.

The reflections—twisted and broken—shrieked.

And then… Sophie stood.

She walked toward the mirror, holding the old music box that had appeared in her double's hands.

"I remember now," she said softly. "This was mine. I brought it here. It was... it was hers. My sister's. She... she died the year before. I thought maybe... if this place was haunted..."

The others stared.

Sophie smiled sadly. "I'm the reason we came. I begged you guys. Jake didn't force anyone. I wanted to come. I thought ghosts were real. I thought I'd see her again."

The mirror was shaking.

Sarah cried out, "Stop! Don't give it anything! That's what it wants!"

But Sophie didn't stop.

"I'm not giving you a memory," she said to the mirror. "I'm letting it go."

She wound the music box.

A haunting lullaby filled the chamber.

And the shadows froze.

One by one, the mirror reflections shattered—starting with Sophie's, then Jake's, Max's, Sarah's.

The music box stopped.

The mirror let out a terrible groan.

Then—it shattered into dust.

The silence afterward was absolute.

Then Max coughed. "Okay. Can we never go into a room with mirrors again?"

Jake reached for Sophie, who leaned into him and clung tight.

Sarah looked around. "Did we... beat it?"

"No," Jake said, still holding Sophie. "We passed its test. For now."

They stood together in the ruins of the mirror chamber—scarred, shaken, and very much alive.

For now.

The Dining Room of
the Damned

It started with a stomach growl

Not just any growl—a guttural, monstrous sound that echoed off the walls like a beast lurking just behind them.

Max clutched his belly and groaned dramatically. "I swear if I don't eat something soon, I'll willingly let the next ghost chew me into ghost nuggets."

Sophie raised an eyebrow. "That's dark. Even for you."

"I'm just saying," Max sniffed. "At this point, a demon fondue sounds better than starving."

Jake gave a tired laugh, his arm still around Sophie. "Careful. This place might take you up on that."

They'd been wandering for what felt like hours since the mirror shattered. The air had changed. It was heavier—damp and oddly warm. The wallpaper peeled in long, curling strips. The lights flickered dimmer than ever.

Sarah clutched her flashlight like a weapon. "Does it feel like the mansion's... shifting?"

Jake nodded. "Yeah. Like it knows we're getting close to something."

"Closer to what?" Max demanded. "Certain death? The exit? A surprise birthday party thrown by ghosts? Because I'd literally take any of those."

Then they smelled it.

Roasted something. Garlic. Butter. Warm bread.

Sophie's eyes widened. "Is that... food?"

Sarah's nose wrinkled. "Okay, either this haunted house has a very confused butler, or we're being lured."

Jake shrugged. "We've walked into at least three cursed rooms already. Might as well add 'evil kitchen' to the bucket list."

Following the scent, they turned a corner and stopped in front of two massive double doors—ornate and decorated with carvings of what looked suspiciously like... forks stabbing screaming people.

Max's hand hovered near the handle. "I know I say this a lot, but this might be the dumbest idea yet."

Sophie gave a tiny smile. "I mean, it is chapter ten. Feels like time for a dinner party."

Jake pushed open the doors.

The dining room stretched out in front of them like something out of an oil painting. A long table ran the length of the chamber, draped in deep crimson cloth. Candles floated above it, flickering softly, casting unsettling shadows that danced like puppets.

And the food...

Golden-roasted chicken, piles of creamy mashed potatoes, glowing wine goblets, steaming pies.

It looked divine.

Too divine.

Sarah took one look and said flatly, "Nope."

Max was already three steps in. "Yes."

Jake held him back by the hoodie. "Let's just look first."

A single chair scraped backward at the head of the table.

Then a voice—silky, male, unmistakably British and deeply unsettling—echoed around the chamber:

"Dinner is served."

A man materialized in the seat. His suit was sharp. His eyes, silver. And his smile? Very likely the original blueprint for all nightmare grins.

He gestured politely. "Please. Sit. You've had a long journey."

Sophie stepped forward. "Who are you?"

"Just the host." His voice poured like warm wine. "You've been such delightful guests. How could I not offer... sustenance?"

Max's stomach rumbled again.

Jake whispered, "It's a trap."

Max whispered back, "I know. But it smells like roasted euphoria."

The host chuckled. "Not a trap. A test. You've passed so many. Survived so much. This... is merely an intermission."

Sarah folded her arms. "What happens if we don't eat?"

The host's smile grew wider. "Then... the feast will eat you."

The table creaked.

Roasted chickens blinked. Mashed potatoes shifted, bubbling like lava. A turkey turned its head and quacked like a duck.

Max recoiled. "Oh my god it's like a Food Network horror movie."

Then, cutlery began to move—forks clicking together like teeth, knives twitching with bloodlust.

Jake yelled, "Okay, no intermission, we're leaving!"

But the doors slammed shut behind them.

The host stood slowly. "One must eat. One must savor. One must serve."

Sophie threw a wine goblet at his head.

It went right through—and splashed against the far wall.

"Great," Sarah muttered. "We're fighting Haunted Gordon Ramsay."

Suddenly, the chairs lunged forward. Forks leapt into the air like javelins. The food jumped—literally—some pies sprouted claws.

The team scattered.

Jake flipped a table, shielding Sophie. "We need to destroy the source!"

"The food?!" Max yelled, karate-chopping a rogue baguette.

"No! Him!" Jake pointed at the host.

Sarah pulled a candelabra from the wall and lit a pie on fire. It screeched. "Is it weird that I'm starting to enjoy this?!"

Max whacked a chicken with a chair leg. "This one's trying to peck my soul out!"

Sophie, breathless, looked around—and saw a painting above the fireplace. It showed the host, younger, mortal, seated at the same table... surrounded by dead guests.

"I think he's bound to the dining room!" she shouted.

Jake tossed her his lighter. "Burn the painting!"

Sophie climbed a chair as it snapped at her ankles. She leapt—landed on the mantel—and set the painting ablaze.

The host screamed.

The food shrieked.

The entire table exploded—gravy, glass, and ghostly smoke filling the air.

And then—silence.

The room was back to normal.

Empty. Cold. Silent.

Sophie collapsed into Jake's arms.

Max wiped gravy from his face. "That... was the most violent Thanksgiving ever."

Sarah shook her head. "This place is insane."

Jake looked around. "We passed another test. But I think it's getting desperate. Or smarter."

Sophie nodded, shivering. "It's trying to break us down. Starve us. Exhaust us. Divide us."

Max groaned. "I'm still hungry."

Jake handed him a squashed granola bar from his pocket. "Make peace with this."

As they stepped out of the dining room, the table behind them flickered back into place. For a moment, the host's eyes reappeared—watching. Smiling.

Then—gone.

XI
The Hall of Lost Promises

They didn't mean to end up there.

One second, they were exiting the cursed dining room, brushing off gravy and near-death experiences. The next, they were standing in a hallway that hadn't been there before.

A long hallway.

Endless, in fact.

And silent—eerily silent, like the mansion was holding its breath.

Sarah took a hesitant step forward. Her boot echoed on the marble floor like it had just smacked a gong. "This doesn't feel right."

Max eyed the corridor's portraits—hundreds of them, all black and white, all of sad-eyed children. "Why is every hallway in this mansion longer than my list of bad life choices?"

Jake whispered, "Don't say that out loud. The house listens."

Sophie rubbed her arms, shivering. "It's cold. Like, funeral-parlor cold."

They began walking, cautiously. The air was thick. The kind of thick that made every breath feel like trying to inhale a nightmare.

Jake stopped suddenly. "Guys..."

They all looked up.

Along the walls were names—etched into the stone, one after another, in neat rows like a school's honor board. But these names weren't of scholars or athletes.

These were the names of the missing.

Amelia Drake.

Peter Vaughn.

Emily Cho.

Sophie Lane.

Sophie froze. "What?"

Max pointed at another. "Jake Morris."

Jake stared. "No. That's not..."

Max Carter. Sarah Monroe. All four names. Burned into the wall.

All four of them were already listed. Like the house had predicted them. Or... remembered them.

"Okay, nope," Max said, backing up. "We are not staying in this creepy Hogwarts detention hallway of doom."

Sarah stepped toward the wall and touched her name. The stone felt warm. Almost like it was breathing beneath her fingers.

Then the hallway changed.

With a sound like cracking ice and crunching bones, the walls slid open—revealing doors.

Each door had a name.

Each door was waiting.

Sophie's voice shook. "Is this another test?"

Jake nodded slowly. "Looks like it. It wants us to go in. Alone."

"Nope," Max said. "I failed solo missions in video games, I'm not failing them in a haunted death tunnel."

But the mansion didn't wait for consensus.

The floor tilted—and suddenly, they were pulled toward their individual doors. Sophie screamed Jake's name. Jake reached out—but too late.

The doors slammed shut behind them.

Inside Sophie's Room:

She found herself in a bedroom.

Her childhood bedroom.

Same posters. Same pink bedsheets. Same crack on the corner of the mirror where she'd thrown her diary in eighth grade.

Except it was perfect. Too perfect.

And sitting on her bed... was her sister.

Lily.

Who died five years ago.

"Hey, Soph," Lily said casually, braiding her hair like it was any normal afternoon. "Wanna go ride bikes? Or sneak out and get candy?"

Sophie's knees buckled. "You're not real."

Lily pouted. "That's rude."

Sophie stepped back. "You're dead. This isn't possible."

"But you wanted to see me again," Lily said, standing now, her voice soft, growing colder. "That's why you brought them to the mansion. For me."

"I didn't—"

"You promised, remember? You said you'd never forget me. But then you stopped visiting my grave. You stopped talking to Mom about me. You forgot."

Sophie's eyes welled with tears. "That's not true."

"You let me die all over again."

The walls darkened. The bed twisted into black vines. Lily's eyes turned hollow. "So now you stay."

Sophie turned and ran—screaming—pounding the door.

Inside Jake's Room:

He was outside the mansion.

Except—it was then. Ten years ago.

He was eight again.

And standing in front of the broken gate.

Sophie was holding his hand. Max was crying. Sarah was limping. They were all kids again.

"Come on!" Young Jake shouted to the others. "We have to go back and help!"

"But the woman said—" Young Max began.

"We made a promise!" Jake cried. "To each other! We said we'd never leave anyone behind!"

He watched his past self run back toward the house. But this time, he didn't follow. He stood frozen.

And beside him, the pale woman appeared again.

Her voice was like silk being torn.

"Jake. You didn't save them. You saved yourself."

"I tried," Jake whispered.

She leaned in close. "But you always knew. You were the first to forget. The first to run."

Then she touched his heart. "And soon, you'll be the first to die."

Inside Max's Room:

It was his father's study.

Old leather chair. Whiskey on the table. Rain outside the window.

And his father—stern, cold, unreadable—sat before him.

"You always joke, Max," the man said, pouring a drink. "Always laugh. Because you're too scared to face who you really are."

Max clenched his fists. "You're not real."

"I'm exactly what you see when you close your eyes," his father replied.

"You're a memory," Max growled. "And you don't scare me anymore."

His father rose. "Then why do you still hear my voice when you mess up? When you feel worthless?"

Max stepped forward, trembling but defiant. "Because I haven't dealt with you. But I'm starting now."

The room shattered.

Inside Sarah's Room:

She was in a church.

Empty pews. Candlelight. A casket at the front.

Her name was engraved on the side.

She backed up. "No. No. I'm not dead."

From the pulpit, a preacher spoke. "You promised to be perfect. To protect everyone. To never make a mistake."

She saw her mother in the front row, weeping.

"You let them down," the preacher said. "You always do."

Sarah screamed. "I'm not perfect! And I'm done pretending!"

The casket exploded into dust. The room burned white.

And then—all four of them woke up.

Lying in the hallway.

Back where they started.

Breathless. Sweating. Pale.

The doors were gone. So were the names.

Max sat up first. "Anyone else have a deeply traumatic emotional panic attack just now?"

Jake groaned. "Yep."

Sophie nodded silently, her eyes red.

Sarah wiped her tears. "It made us face what we feared most. What we promised never to confront."

Jake looked at all of them. "But we're still here."

Max tried to smile. "Okay, new rule—no one ever promises anything ever again. Not even to finish each other's fries."

Sophie actually giggled. "Deal."

They stood slowly, bruised and exhausted, but closer than ever.

Whatever the mansion threw at them next—they weren't facing it alone.

XII

The Screaming Stairs

The mansion had changed again.

As in... literally rearranged itself.

One second they were catching their breath after that mind-melting hallway from hell, and the next they were standing in front of a velvet curtain that hadn't been there before. Floor tiles shifted beneath their feet like a giant had shaken the house, and distant moans pulsed through the walls like something was crawling inside them.

Jake steadied himself against the wall. "Okay. I'm pretty sure the house is now actively trying to digest us."

"Awesome," Max muttered. "We're ghost chow."

Sophie was staring at the curtain. Her voice was barely a whisper. "It's breathing."

They turned. Sure enough—it was.

The curtain rose and fell rhythmically, as though it covered the lungs of the house itself.

Sarah narrowed her eyes. "I think it wants us to go in."

"I think it wants to inhale us," Max said, stepping back.

"Maybe it's just trying to be dramatic," Jake offered, forcing a grin. "You know. Theater kids meet demon lair."

"Yeah?" Sophie shot back. "Well, I'd rather deal with a demon musical than another door showing me my dead sister."

That shut everyone up.

Jake gently took Sophie's hand, quietly grounding her. She didn't pull away.

Sarah stepped forward. "We're not dying here. We go together. We leave together."

Max sighed. "Why do I feel like this is going to involve tentacles?"

Sophie shrugged. "Because statistically, it always does."

And with that, they pulled the curtain aside.

The room beyond was... breathing.

Not the curtain. The room.

Its walls slowly pulsed in and out like lungs. The wallpaper was made of some kind of leathery fabric that flexed and released, and the ceiling oozed a translucent sweat that shimmered with faint screams.

There were no light bulbs—just glowing veins running through the ceiling, casting the room in a reddish, biological glow. It was like stepping inside a living creature's chest cavity.

"Okay," Max whispered. "So, we're inside a stomach. A haunted stomach. Fantastic."

Jake nodded. "I hate how you're probably right."

In the center of the room sat a table. A dinner table, just like the one in the haunted dining room. But this one was different.

This one... was set for four.

Each place had a name card. Jake. Sophie. Sarah. Max.

Each plate was full. With food.

If you could call it that.

Max's plate had what looked like a burger... until it blinked.

Jake's had spaghetti that slithered across the china like it was trying to escape.

Sophie's held a cake shaped like a heart. A real heart. It was beating.

Sarah's plate was the worst—just a mirror. Her own face staring back.

Jake backed away. "I'm not hungry."

"Too bad," came a voice.

It was the mansion. The walls vibrated with it. Soft. Calm. Amused.

"You will eat. Or you will starve. Choose."

The doors behind them slammed shut.

Max threw a fork. "WE'RE ON A DIET, YOU SICK WALLPAPER!"

The room shook with laughter. The food began to rot on the plates—fast. Maggots, slime, decay. The smell hit them like a physical slap.

Sarah gagged, clutching her stomach. "We need to get out of here."

Sophie ran to the door, yanked it—it didn't budge. She pounded on it.

The voice came again. Louder.

"You left once before. You broke the promise. Not again."

The walls pulsed harder. From behind the dinner table, the floor cracked open—and something climbed out.

It looked like a child.

No—four children.

Tiny, pale, black-eyed copies of them.

Mini Jake. Mini Max. Mini Sarah. Mini Sophie.

Jake stumbled back. "Are those... us?"

The mini versions smiled. Then their mouths opened—way too wide.

And they started to scream.

Not normal screams.

Screams that cut through the air like knives. That reached inside their heads and pulled at old, buried memories. The room bent under the pressure—walls vibrating, the floor cracking open, lights dimming to a pulse.

Sarah fell to her knees. "It's trying to break us apart again! It's showing us what we used to be!"

"No," Jake gritted out. "It's showing us what we lost. The childhood we forgot."

Max was pale. "I remember this. That thing... it was us. We were here. When we were kids."

Jake's voice cracked. "We didn't find this house on accident."

The room exploded with laughter.

"Now you remember."

Sophie's eyes widened. "We came here. When we were little. We got in. And something went wrong."

Sarah looked like she'd been punched. "The house erased our memories."

Max groaned. "Oh my god... are we ghost bait?"

The mini versions stopped screaming. They turned their heads in sync toward the group. Then, together, they said:

"The promise was to never forget."

And they leapt.

Mini-Jake tackled Jake, biting his arm. Jake yelped, throwing him off.

Mini-Max clawed at Max's face, laughing like a deranged hyena.

Mini-Sarah floated in the air, eyes glowing white. She screamed a single word: "LIAR."

Mini-Sophie grinned. "We remember. You chose to forget. Now you pay."

Jake scrambled to the table and grabbed a candleholder. He swung it like a baseball bat, knocking Mini-Jake across the room.

"GET TO THE CENTER!" he shouted. "There's a trap door!"

Max flipped Mini-Max into a bowl of brain-mashed potatoes and ran. "I hate demon me!"

Sarah ran to Sophie, pulling her toward the center. The floor was cracking open again—deeper this time. Like a throat. Or a chute.

"I'm not jumping into that!" Sophie yelled.

"Do you want to wait for your evil clone to eat you?!" Sarah screamed.

"Fair point."

Jake grabbed her hand. Max dove in.

Then Sarah.

Then Sophie.

Jake turned one last time. The room was closing.

The mini versions stood in a circle, staring.

Jake met their gaze.

"I didn't forget," he whispered. "I just didn't want to remember."

Then he jumped.

They fell.

Like skydiving through darkness.

Time bent. Space screamed. Light flickered.

They landed—hard—on cold tile.

For a second, no one moved.

Then Sophie groaned. "Okay. New rule. No more rooms that breathe."

Max rolled onto his back. "Or talk. Or eat people. Or clone us."

Jake sat up, rubbing his elbow. "Or remind us of emotional trauma we buried with cartoons and sarcasm."

Sarah blinked.

They were in a new room.

Stone walls. A ceiling covered in hundreds of candles—floating.

It was like a cathedral had been swallowed by a volcano.

At the center of the room... stood a mirror.

Tall. Ancient. Black glass.

Sophie whispered, "This isn't over, is it?"

Jake shook his head. "Nope."

Max sighed. "Okay. So what next? More trauma? More creepy kids? More rooms that feel like your ex's personality?"

Sarah pointed to the mirror.

And in the glass—they saw something moving.

But it wasn't their reflection.

It was the past.

Them. As children. Running. Screaming. Holding hands.

Being chased by something... with teeth.

Sophie's voice cracked. "It wasn't just one trip. We came here every year. Until..."

She trailed off.

Max's jaw clenched. "Until someone didn't make it back."

Jake's heart stopped.

The mirror whispered.

"You forgot the fifth."

XIII

Echoes of the
Forgotten

The morning sun filtered weakly through the thick jungle canopy, casting fractured patterns of light and shadow over the four friends as they stepped cautiously along the dirt path. The mansion had vanished, erased from the world like a bad dream—but the weight of what they'd uncovered in the depths of that final chamber still clung to them, thick and heavy.

Jake, Sophie, Max, and Sarah walked in silence, each lost in their own tangled thoughts, the echoes of Isaac's voice lingering like a whispered promise.

Jake's grip on Sophie's hand tightened, as if grounding himself in reality. "We're back," he said quietly, almost to convince himself.

"But is it really 'back'?" Max asked, eyes scanning the trees suspiciously. "Feels like we jumped into some alternate dimension where everything's... wrong."

Sarah shivered, rubbing her arms. "The mansion's gone, sure. But the way the jungle smells—like burnt wood and something else... I don't know, it's like the house left a stain on everything."

Sophie swallowed hard, trying to shake the chill creeping up her spine. "We remembered Isaac. The past. That fire... the pact we never knew we made. I don't think the mansion was just a place. It was a trap. A prison for us, for him."

Jake glanced over his shoulder, half-expecting to see the mansion's twisted silhouette lurking behind the trees. But all that stretched out was jungle, humming with the indifferent sounds of cicadas and rustling leaves.

A sudden rustle in the underbrush made them all jump.

Max held up a finger, signaling silence.

Out from the greenery emerged a figure—not ghostly this time—but very much alive.

It was a woman.

Tall, slender, with piercing green eyes and tangled black hair that caught the sunlight like dark silk. She wore a worn leather jacket and carried a satchel that looked like it held years of secrets.

She stopped just a few feet away, studying the group with an unreadable expression.

"Finally," she said softly, voice like gravel and honey mixed.

Jake took a cautious step forward. "Who are you?"

The woman smiled thinly. "I'm someone who's been watching. Waiting for you to remember. You're not the first to stumble into the mansion's curse, but you might be the last."

Sophie's brows knit together. "What do you mean, 'last'? And how do you know about the mansion?"

The woman's eyes darkened. "Because I lost someone there too."

Sarah's eyes widened. "Lost? Like Isaac?"

"Exactly like Isaac," the woman said, nodding. "My brother, Marcus. He disappeared inside the mansion years ago. Like you kids, I thought it was a nightmare I could escape. But the mansion never lets go."

Max glanced at Jake, a flicker of doubt crossing his face. "So what? You want to help us? Or are you just another ghost story?"

The woman stepped closer, her gaze steady. "I'm here because you've reopened something. The pact Isaac spoke of—it's not just a curse on the mansion. It's on all of us. On anyone who's touched that place."

Jake's heart pounded. "What kind of pact?"

She pulled out an old, cracked journal from her satchel, flipping it open. The pages were filled with hurried handwriting, sketches of the mansion, strange symbols.

"The house feeds on memories," she explained. "It traps souls by erasing what they hold dear, then lures them back to pay the price."

Sophie's voice was barely a whisper. "So we're trapped again?"

"Not yet," the woman replied. "But the longer you stay in this twisted reality, the stronger the mansion's grip becomes."

Sarah took a deep breath. "Then what do we do? How do we break free for good?"

The woman smiled sadly. "You need to find the Heart of the mansion. The source of its power. Destroy it. But beware—the mansion will fight back harder than ever."

Jake's jaw clenched. "We've come this far. We're not turning back now."

The woman nodded. "Good. Because this is just the beginning."

As she spoke, the jungle around them began to shift. The trees grew taller, shadows lengthened unnaturally, and a cold wind whispered through the leaves, carrying voices—soft, beckoning, dangerous.

Max gulped. "Yeah... I definitely don't like this."

Sophie stepped closer to Jake. "Whatever happens, we stick together. No more secrets."

Jake nodded, squeezing her hand. "No more secrets."

The woman closed the journal. "Then follow me. Time is running out."

Together, they plunged deeper into the jungle, toward a destiny that would test every ounce of their courage, friendship, and love.

But none of them could guess what waited in the darkness ahead...

XIV

The Heart of Shadows

The jungle seemed alive around them, breathing and whispering secrets with every rustle of the leaves. The woman who called herself Lena led the way, her footsteps light but purposeful, carving a path through the dense undergrowth. The air was thick, humid, and heavy with a smell neither fresh nor rotten, but somewhere in between—like the scent of old secrets trapped beneath moss and stone.

Jake, Sophie, Max, and Sarah followed closely, their nerves prickling with every crack of a twig or distant bird call that felt oddly wrong—too sharp, too sudden.

Sophie broke the silence. "How do you know so much about the mansion? How did you survive?"

Lena's eyes darkened. "I didn't. Not really. I escaped once, but the mansion's shadow followed me. The curse isn't just walls and fire—it's memories, regrets, unfinished business."

Sarah swallowed. "So you're like us... trapped by the past?"

Lena nodded slowly. "Exactly. And the only way out is to face it head-on."

Max scowled. "That sounds awful. And also, kind of like a bad horror movie cliché."

Jake cracked a small smile. "Well, we've been living a horror movie, Max. Might as well star in the finale."

The group reached a clearing. In the center stood a massive ancient tree, its bark blackened and twisted as if scorched by fire but still pulsing with a faint golden light from within its gnarled roots.

Lena stopped and pointed. "The Heart. The source of the mansion's power. Destroy that, and the curse breaks."

Jake stepped forward, eyes locked on the glowing roots. "Easy to say, but how do we destroy it?"

Lena pulled from her satchel a small, ornate dagger, its blade inscribed with symbols that shimmered faintly. "This. It was forged from the last iron found near the mansion's foundation. It can sever the bonds the mansion uses to trap souls."

Sophie swallowed her fear and stepped beside Jake. "Then let's end this nightmare."

They approached the tree. The golden glow grew brighter, casting long shadows across their faces. Suddenly, the ground trembled. From the shadows around the clearing, twisted shapes emerged—ghostly figures, their faces contorted in silent screams, reaching out with spectral hands.

"Guardians," Lena whispered urgently. "They protect the Heart."

Max groaned. "Figures."

The friends braced themselves, ready to fight, hearts pounding like drums in the oppressive silence.

Sophie felt Jake's hand on hers, grounding her. "Together," he whispered.

The ghostly forms surged forward, swirling like smoke and ash. Sophie dodged a grasp, her breath hitching as cold fingers brushed her arm. Max swung a fallen branch like a club, but it passed through the apparition harmlessly.

Jake raised the dagger, its blade gleaming. "I'll distract them. You find a way to cut the roots."

Sarah scanned the roots, eyes sharp. "There! If we cut the glowing tendrils, the Heart should collapse."

Lena nodded. "I'll cover you."

Jake charged, the dagger flashing like lightning. The ghosts recoiled, hissing, their forms solidifying into twisted versions of the kids' own faces — mocking, angry, desperate.

Jake's voice rang out: "You won't keep us trapped!"

With a fierce swing, he slashed through a spectral figure, which dissolved into sparks.

Sophie, Max, and Sarah scrambled to the roots, using knives, broken branches, and anything sharp. The glowing tendrils hissed and writhed as they were severed one by one, the golden light dimming.

But the guardians' attacks grew fiercer.

One reached for Sophie, icy cold wrapping around her wrist. Panic surged.

Jake yelled, "Hold on!"

With a mighty roar, Jake lunged into the fray, cutting down the closest specters, his every move precise, fueled by desperation and courage.

Suddenly, the ground beneath Jake cracked and glowed bright.

The Heart pulsed violently.

Lena's voice cut through the chaos. "Jake, no!"

Too late.

The roots surged upward, wrapping around Jake's legs, holding him fast.

Jake grinned fiercely. "Looks like I'm part of the show now."

"No!" Sophie screamed, struggling against the ghosts.

Jake raised the dagger, eyes locked with hers. "Finish this. Break the curse. Save us all."

Tears blurred Sophie's vision as she slashed the last glowing tendril. The Heart exploded in a burst of golden light, shattering the roots and dissolving the guardians.

Jake collapsed, the bindings released but his strength fading.

Sarah and Max caught him.

Lena knelt beside Jake, eyes wet. "You saved us."

Jake smiled faintly. "Sometimes... you have to be the sacrifice to set everyone free."

Sophie held his hand tightly. "Don't say that."

Jake's eyes closed, a peaceful smile on his lips as the golden light surrounded him, lifting him slowly into the air.

The curse was broken.

But at a price.

XV

The Last Light

'The jungle held its breath.

A suffocating silence wrapped around them as the last echoes of the golden explosion faded into the humid air. The Heart of the mansion—the sinister core that had fed on their fears, their pain, and their very souls—was shattered, but its destruction left a wound far deeper than anyone could have imagined.

Jake lay cradled in Sophie's arms, pale as the moonlight that filtered through the dense canopy above. His chest rose and fell with shallow, uneven breaths, as if the life was slipping through him like sand in an hourglass. His usually vibrant eyes were dim, flickering with the faintest spark of something untouchable, a ghost of the boy they had all known.

Sophie's fingers trembled against his clammy skin. "Jake... you're going to be okay," she whispered, though her voice broke under the weight of doubt.

Jake's lips twitched into a weak smile, so fragile it could have been mistaken for a flicker of a dying candle. "I'm sorry," he breathed, voice barely audible over the heavy thrum of the jungle. "I never wanted this... for any of us."

Max stood stiff, jaw clenched tight enough to hurt, eyes burning with a mixture of anger and disbelief. "No. You're not allowed to give up. Not now."

Sarah crouched beside them, clutching Jake's hand as if sheer will could pull him back from the edge. "There has to be a way to save him. There has to be."

Sophie shook her head, tears streaming unbidden down her cheeks. "He saved us. He fought the darkness... and now it's taking him."

The jungle around them seemed to mourn, as though the trees and vines themselves sensed the fragility of the moment. Leaves rustled softly, whispering mournful secrets on the humid breeze.

Jake's eyes fluttered open again, locking with Sophie's. "You... you have to keep going. Promise me. Promise you'll live."

"No," Sophie sobbed. "Not without you."

His fingers brushed her cheek, weak but warm. "You'll carry me with you. In your heart. The mansion... it can't touch that."

A distant sound echoed—a soft, haunting melody carried on the wind. Sophie's breath hitched. It was a song she recognized but couldn't place—a lullaby from a memory erased by the mansion's curse, one she thought forever lost.

Max's voice broke through the quiet. "Jake, we're not leaving you. We survive together, or we don't survive at all."

Jake's smile faltered, pain flashing behind his eyes. "You have to. I'm the price. The curse is broken because of me."

Sarah tightened her grip on his hand. "That's not fair."

Jake's voice was barely a whisper. "Life... isn't."

For a long moment, the four friends sat frozen, the jungle pressing in on all sides as the sun dipped low, casting long shadows that seemed to stretch endlessly.

Then, as twilight deepened, Sophie leaned down and pressed a kiss to Jake's forehead, tasting the salt of her own tears. "I love you," she whispered fiercely. "I'm not ready to say goodbye."

Jake's breathing slowed further, his body growing still. Yet the faint smile lingered, a testament to the hope he carried beyond the darkness.

Jake's fingers, once interlaced tightly with Sophie's, began to slacken. She leaned closer, her sobs shaking her body, unwilling to let go.

"Jake," Sophie whispered again, "Don't do this. Don't leave me. You still owe me a date, remember?"

That earned the smallest twitch at the corner of Jake's mouth.

"Rain check?" he rasped.

Sophie let out a strangled laugh through her tears. "Only if you actually show up this time."

"I will..." His voice was fading, barely a whisper. "Every time it rains."

There was a pause, a long, emotional silence. Sophie leaned closer, thinking those were his last words. Then—Jake blinked slowly, drew in one last ragged breath, and with a crooked grin said:

"...And the Chrome history is not mine."

Max froze. Sarah's mouth fell open. Sophie choked out a laugh mid-sob, tears still falling.

"You stupid idiot," she cried, half-laughing, half-screaming through her grief.

Jake's grin didn't fade. It stayed with him even as the last light in his eyes dimmed, like he wanted to go out not just with love—but with one last joke, one last punchline.

Then... he was still.

Where Jake goes:

Immediately after his death, the jungle pulses. A soft golden mist rises from Jake's chest. It's his soul — his essence — not consumed by the mansion, but released. It doesn't just vanish.

Instead, it spreads outward, washing over the others. It restores their erased childhood memories, heals some of their emotional scars, and leaves a piece of Jake behind with each of them — like his spirit is choosing to remain within them, not trapped in the haunted world.

Then, the mist ascends into the trees and sky, not as a soul being dragged to an afterlife, but as one being freed, unshackled, and at peace.

Jake doesn't go to the mansion. He doesn't get absorbed by darkness.

He goes into memory. Into legacy. Into them.

And every time it rains... they'll know he's still close.

Sophie wiped her face as the golden mist that once was Jake shimmered around them like living memory. It didn't vanish. It lingered, like it was soaking into their bones, their blood, their story.

She could feel it — not just the grief, but the warmth of every inside joke, every dumb prank, every stupid bet he made. He was still there. Not haunting them, but anchored in them. Alive in laughter.

Max stood, swallowing hard. "He'd say something like, 'Quit crying, you emotional waffles. I'm fine.'"

Sarah nodded, her voice barely holding together. "And then he'd probably fart and say it was ghost air."

The three of them laughed, the sound cracked but real. It echoed through the clearing — a sound the mansion hadn't heard in centuries. Laughter that came from love, not madness.

Then the jungle shuddered.

Leaves rattled. The ground pulsed again. But this time, it wasn't death rolling in — it was release. A deep, final exhale from the land itself.

Somewhere in the distance, the mansion groaned. The walls of the cursed house, now buried beneath roots and time, gave one last wail before splitting open at the seams. A burst of white-blue energy exploded from its core, tearing the sky above it like fabric. A flash — brilliant and blinding — washed over the jungle, and then...

Silence.

And when it faded — no mansion. No shadows. No curse.

Just forest. Just rain.

Max blinked. "Is it... is it gone?"

Sophie stared at the space where it had been. "It's over."

They didn't wait for another shift. Didn't risk another whisper from the void.

They lifted Jake's body gently, wrapping him in Max's overshirt and Sophie's trembling hands. They carried him through the clearing, past the trees that had once clawed at them like living beasts. Now the vines simply parted, guiding them. The jungle was clearing its throat, preparing to let them go.

Hours passed — or maybe minutes, time was impossible to hold in a place like this — and eventually, they stepped into the sunlight.

They were out.

And the road, now visible again, stretched out toward civilization.

The moment they passed the last tree, the mist that had clung to Jake floated free, glowing brighter for a second... then dissolving gently into the wind, as if whispering:

"Remember me stupidly."

One week later – in the town of Eldridge Falls...

The three survivors stood at the edge of the school parking lot.

Except it wasn't the same school.

The sign still read "Eldridge High," but the font was different. The school was three floors now instead of two. The brick was darker. And when Sophie asked a passing student if they'd heard of Jake...

They shrugged.

"Jake who?"

Max checked his phone — no texts from Jake. Not even old ones. His entire thread was gone.

Sarah had pulled up Jake's social media.

Nothing. No account.

No trace.

It was like the world had moved on without him — or worse, rewritten itself to forget he ever existed.

Sophie's heart pounded. "This doesn't make sense. He was here. He was real. We all—"

"He is real," Max cut in. "He's in here." He tapped his chest. "Screw this weird reset reality. We don't forget. That's how we win."

Sarah looked up. "What if the mansion didn't disappear... it just changed?"

They turned.

Behind them, down the street, a house stood that hadn't been there yesterday. It looked perfectly normal — like a modern suburban home with red shutters and a picket fence.

But the paint was peeling. The door was ajar.

And something about it felt familiar.

Max whispered, "No. No freaking way."

Sophie took a step forward. "It's watching us."

Sarah added, "Or waiting."

And then, as if responding to them, the house's upstairs window swung open. A gust of cold air hit their backs.

On the inside of the glass... someone had drawn a smiley face with their finger.

The exact kind Jake used to leave on foggy windows.

Three dots. Two slanted eyes. And a tongue sticking out.

Sophie laughed — the sound short and breathless.

Sarah shook her head. "You think he's still in there?"

Max nodded, solemnly. "He said he'd show up when it rains."

And behind them, as thunder cracked in the distance, the first drop of rain fell on Sophie's cheek.

She smiled, even through her tears.

Jake was still here.

Not haunting.

Not gone.

Just... waiting for them to laugh again.

[Final lines of the book]

As the rain fell harder, the three idiots turned from the twisted new house and walked toward town.

They didn't look back.

But the house did.

Its windows blinked.

Its doorknob twisted.

And from somewhere deep inside, a low, familiar voice echoed:

"Hey. Don't touch my Chrome history."

Then the house fell silent.

But not for long.

A Few Weeks Later...

Life returned. Sort of.

Sarah rejoined classes, though she didn't laugh as loud anymore — unless Sophie made a terrible pun. Max had taken to wearing Jake's old hoodie like a battle cloak. It didn't fit right, but he never took it off. Sophie wrote more. Filled entire notebooks with scribbled conversations she remembered between the four of them, doodles of Jake sticking his tongue out, a list of dumb things he said (yes, including Chrome history), and an ever-growing page titled:

"Things We'll Say to Him When We See Him Again"

The world outside their trio was clueless. Teachers didn't remember Jake. His locker had someone else's name on it. The jungle they'd found? Now just part of a construction site. Supposedly there had never been a forest there.

Even Google Earth didn't show anything unusual.

But they remembered.

They always would.

And that was what terrified them the most — not just that the mansion had changed reality, but that it hadn't finished.

Two Months Later – Halloween Night

Sophie, Max, and Sarah stood outside the new house again.

It looked... sharper now. Like it had aged overnight. Or remembered what it once was.

The porch light flickered. A jack-o-lantern sat on the step — grinning like Jake.

"Why are we here again?" Sarah whispered. "We survived. We should be halfway through a therapy session or something."

Sophie shrugged. "I just... felt drawn."

Max took out his phone. "I didn't even remember coming here. Like I woke up, and I was walking."

They stared up at the house.

Then the front door creaked open.

Nobody inside.

Just shadow.

No breeze. No kids. No people. Just a yawning doorway full of velvet dark.

Then a sound — slow and familiar — drifted from inside:

Click. Click. Clack.

It was the sound of Jake's old Zippo lighter. The one he'd use to scare them around the campfire. Click-click, flick, clack.

And then... laughter.

His laugh.

Real.

Alive.

But wrong.

Twisted.

Like something else was wearing Jake's laugh now.

Max stepped back. "We need to go."

But Sophie stepped forward. "No. What if he's trapped? What if that... thing is using him?"

Sarah grabbed her hand. "Then we burn that place to hell. Again."

Sophie nodded. "Let's finish what he started."

They stepped inside.

Inside the House

The moment they crossed the threshold, the house swallowed them. Like literally swallowed — the hallway twisted around them like a throat closing.

The door slammed shut.

The walls dripped.

Whispers echoed — but they weren't just ghostly mutters.

They were memories.

Jake's voice:

"Max, put the frog down!"

"Sophie, I swear if you touch my fries again..."

"Sarah, if you hex me one more time with glitter..."

Every memory, every laugh, bouncing off the walls, looping, building — until they sounded distorted. Too fast. Too slow. Then too loud. Until...

Silence.

A spotlight blinked on.

And there, in the center of a room that hadn't existed seconds ago...

Jake.

Standing.

Alive.

Wearing his hoodie. Smiling.

"Sophie," he said softly.

She ran to him.

But Max grabbed her arm.

"Wait—"

Too late.

Jake opened his arms.

She fell into them.

And then froze.

His arms weren't warm.

They were cold.

Too cold.

And when she looked up — his eyes were black.

Not shadowed. Not soulless.

Occupied.

"Jake?" she whispered.

His smile grew wider.

And wider.

His jaw split unnaturally, growing longer, teeth sharper.

"Don't worry," it said in his voice, with a voice behind it. "He's here. Watching."

From above them, the ceiling pulsed. A hundred red eyes opened in the beams.

Jake's body convulsed. The thing inside him flickered in and out of shape. One second it looked like Jake. The next... like something ancient. Something that had been waiting for a new host.

It hadn't let him go.

Jake had held it back at the mansion — used himself to keep it sealed.

But now... it had found a way through.

Max shouted. "Let him go!"

The thing laughed. "He wants this. It was the only way to stay close to you. Didn't you notice the rain always started when I was near?"

Sophie trembled. "You're not him."

"No," the voice said through Jake's mouth. "But you let me in when you kept remembering. That's all I needed."

Then — from deep inside — a whisper:

"Sophie..."

Her eyes widened. That voice.

That was him.

Real Jake. Trapped deep within.

She pulled back.

And stabbed the thing with the one thing she'd kept from the jungle — the broken vine talisman the old woman had given them.

The creature howled.

The house screamed.

Jake's body convulsed and fell limp.

And suddenly — everything broke.

Outside the House – Later

They were on the lawn again.

The house... gone.

No trace.

Not even rubble.

Sophie was sobbing, her hands bloody from the broken talisman. Max and Sarah held her.

And then — the clouds parted.

And a single beam of moonlight hit the grass.

There, shimmering faintly...

Jake.

For real this time.

No monster.

No mansion.

Just Jake.

He looked tired, older, but at peace.

"Sorry," he said, "for the possession. It was... weird."

They laughed.

Max sniffed. "You really do show up when it rains."

Jake grinned. "Told you."

Sophie reached for him — but her hand passed through his.

He winced.

"I can't stay," he said. "You closed the loop. You set me free. But... I'll always be around."

He looked up.

"It's not over, though. That thing — it's not dead. Just buried."

Sarah tilted her head. "Where?"

Jake looked right at the reader.

Then smirked.

"Behind you."

And vanished.

In this book the real adventure was not in the mansion it was in the love in their friendship.

"If you hear laughter in the dark...
Don't turn around.
Jake says hi."
To be continued... ?